ZOMBIE PATROL

THE WALKING PLAGUE TRILOGY

BOOK #1

ZOMBIE PATROL

THE WALKING PLAGUE TRILOGY

BOOK #1

by

J.R. Rain

&

Elizabeth Basque

ISBN-13: 9781482083095
ISBN-10: 1482083094

Other Books by J.R. Rain

STANDALONE NOVELS

The Lost Ark

The Body Departed

Elvis Has *Not* Left the Building

COLLABORATIONS

Cursed! (with Scott Nicholson)

The Vampire Club (with Scott Nicholson)

VAMPIRE FOR HIRE SERIES

Moon Dance

Vampire Moon

American Vampire

Moon Child

Christmas Moon

Vampire Dawn

Vampire Games

Moon Island

SAMANTHA MOON SHORT STORIES

Teeth

Vampire Nights

Vampires Blues

Vampire Dreams

Halloween Moon

JIM KNIGHTHORSE SERIES

Dark Horse

The Mummy Case

Hail Mary

SPINOZA TRILOGY

The Vampire With the Dragon Tattoo

The Vampire Who Played Dead

The Vampire in the Iron Mask

ALADDIN TRILOGY

with Piers Anthony

Aladdin Relighted

Aladdin Sins Bad

Aladdin and the Flying Dutchman

GRAIL QUEST TRILOGY

Arthur

WALKING PLAGUE TRILOGY

with Elizabeth Basque

Zombie Patrol

SPIDER SERIES

with Scott Nicholson and H.T. Night

Bad Blood

NICK CAINE SERIES

with Aiden James

Temple of the Jaguar

GHOST FILES SERIES

edited with Scott Nicholson

Ghost College

Ghost Fire

Ghost Soldier

Ghost Hall

SHORT STORY COLLECTIONS

The Bleeder and Other Stories

Vampires Rain and Other Stories

The Santa Call: A Christmas Story

SCREENPLAYS

Judas Silver: The Screenplay

Lost Eden: The Screenplay

Other Books by Elizabeth Basque

Sharpened Edges

The Vampire in the Iron Mask

Zombie Patrol

Dedication

The authors dedicate this book to Night and Day.
That is, H.T. Night and P.J. Day.

CHAPTER ONE

I knelt in the prickly brush on the hillside and carefully took aim. The cougar sniffed the air, but I was downwind. About twenty yards away, Anna watched intently from the truck. I knew she hated this part, but she kept still and very quiet. As did I.

The cougar sensed another presence besides her two cubs, but I had been doing this kind of thing for years. I knew to wait for the right moment. I gauged her at about seventy-five pounds; not too big for a wildcat. Actually, she looked thin. Probably hungry, too; these beasts didn't come near civilization unless necessary. She'd probably wandered here from Griffith Park in search of food for herself and her two cubs, so I wasn't absolutely sure just how strong she was.

The best place to hit her was in the back of the neck, so I waited for her to turn to the right position. She growled a little as one of the cubs tugged playfully at her tail. She was in no mood for play—she was very intuitive. I could tell. This cougar was nothing to fool around with.

Suddenly, she glanced in my direction. I held my breath. I knew Anna did, too. The cougar's long, direct gaze penetrated me. I was ready to pull the trigger if she so much as hinted at a move in my direction. I didn't blink, I didn't move. I waited. She waited.

It was pre-dawn, still almost dark. Her vision was pretty much perfect in such light. Mine, not so much. She stood stone-still, watching me from slightly higher ground.

As quickly as she'd focused on me, she released her gaze and bent to sniff the ground.

I mouthed a word of prayer, and then...I pulled the trigger, launching the dart into the back of her neck. I quickly shot her again, this time between her shoulder blades. The cat screeched and ran, her cubs following obediently. I followed, as well. I knew Anna was dying to get out of the truck, but I signaled for her to wait a little longer.

One just never knew how tranquilizers would affect a wildcat. I hoped my aim was true and that this one would go down quickly. As I reloaded my injection rifle, I rushed through the foliage, following her tracks. How I didn't trip and fall on my face, I don't know. I hated leaving Anna alone in the truck, but I was wearing protective arm shields as well as a vest. Anna only had the vest, and even then, it was a little too big for her.

I found the old girl some thirty yards further up the hillside, struggling to stay on her feet. I silently thanked the gods for the anesthesia's speed, even though she hissed viciously. Her cubs were a little bewildered. They watched with curiosity as I slowly approached. Mama usually told them what to do but Mama was staggering now, darts hanging from her neck and back.

As soon as the cat went down, I heard the truck door slam. There was a quiet rustle from the back of the truck, and then, shortly, Anna was beside me, out of breath and smelling like perfume. Who wore perfume on a tagging mission? Either way, I was grateful that she'd insisted on wearing moccasins. Hell, she could move as quietly as this cat.

Our work here wasn't done, not by a long shot. I glanced over at the cage she'd carried with her. Anna looked up at me for approval. She always sought my approval, although she had already earned it the moment she was born. I almost winced at her beauty. Instead, I smiled and nodded a little. Her replying angelic grin made me glad I'd brought her along.

The cubs were still small, so I let Anna work on them as I bound the cougar's paws, front and back. My volunteer co-worker sat cross-legged on the ground, distracting the cubs and coaxing them closer, the cage not far away. They were wary. They wanted to stay near their mother. Anna scooted a little closer. She'd covered her hands with earth, as I had, to try to mask our human scent. It worked a little. Her easy spirit worked better.

My work done, I watched silently as Anna worked her magic. She held a branch in one hand, moving it back and forth on the ground in a teasing motion. She held out her other dirt-covered hand, face up. Neither of us spoke. She merely held the cubs' eyes and urged them to her. Slowly, slowly, they inched closer, spellbound by my daughter. She got them to play with the branch, and somehow, she maneuvered them closer to the cage, which was now also lined with branches.

I stopped breathing again when one cub climbed onto her lap. This was a critical time, and Anna knew it as well as I did. If either of us showed a hint of fear, these wild cubs would pick up on it and flee. I looked at my watch. It was probably another fifteen to twenty minutes until the mother would stir. I still hadn't radioed the zoo, and there wasn't much time unless I injected the mother again, which I didn't want to do. Anna knew all this. Now, it was my turn to wait.

With one cub in her lap, she placed the branch nearer to the cage. With both hands now free, she toyed with the first cub as the second approached cautiously. Finally, it came close enough for her to grasp. Quick as lightning, she gripped each cub by the scruffs of their necks and slipped them carefully into the cage. I was by her side in an instant and, much to the cougar cubs' dismay, we closed and locked the door.

Anna sat back and sighed. "Whew!" She laughed, and regarded the two cubs mischievously. "I got you two buggers."

The cubs cried for their mother as Anna cooed at them through the metal cage. I switched on my radio. I watched my fourteen-year-old daughter with renewed awe as I talked into the walkie-talkie.

"Brice," I said.

"That you, Carter?" came the voice over some static.

"Ten-four. I've got your cougar here."

"You kiddin' me?"

I turned to the mother cougar, presently lying on her side. "I'm not," I responded, "and there isn't much time."

Anna left the cubs and gingerly approached the big cat. My hand reached for the rifle. Anna shook her head at me in defiance as I motioned for her to keep her distance.

I gave Brice our location in the north hills surrounding the zoo. "Can you be here within ten minutes?" I asked. I was beside Anna now. She caressed the mother's injection sites. She ignored my motions to stop. She didn't even have gloves on.

"Christ on a Christmas tree, Jack! Ten minutes?"

"I don't want to sedate her again if we can help it," the words spilled out before I could retract them. Too late. *Oops.*

"We? You've got Anna with you *again*?"

I could already imagine Brice's disapproving frown. I didn't have time to reply before his words vomited loudly through the walkie-talkie—too loudly.

"How many times do I have to tell you, Jack Carter," he snapped, "that having her assist with any animal rescue is *illegal.* The liability alone—"

"This is her last time," I said. "I swear."

"That's what you said last time."

"Look, let's talk about it later. I presently have a sleeping wildcat on my hands—a cat that's gonna be very, very pissed off in twenty minutes. Besides," I added.

"Besides what?" snapped Brice.

"My daughter is a natural," I said proudly.

CHAPTER TWO

On the day that changed his life forever, Lieutenant Commander Joseph Carter fought anxiety as he veered his government vehicle off the freeway.

He headed toward the naval base in Seal Beach, pondering who and what awaited him. He knew he wasn't supposed to smoke in the car. He lit a cigarette anyway. He told himself that he hadn't done anything wrong. Nothing to worry about. But still...

Why had he been summoned?

"You know why," he told himself, but he didn't want to think about it now. He inhaled deeply, turned up the radio and opened the car's windows to clear out the tobacco smoke.

The base was less than ten minutes from the freeway. That meant, the Lieutenant Commander told himself, that he had ten minutes to gather his thoughts. Not that he hadn't been doing so since earlier today when he was first ordered to report to Seal Beach. He wasn't feeling well, and his sunglasses did little to shield the blinding rays that made his head ache even worse. He had little appetite. No surprise there. This morning, he'd consumed about a half-gallon of water, which he'd later upchucked.

"Must be the flu," he muttered, remembering that his buddy, Mike, had displayed the same symptoms. Thinking of Mike, he glanced in his rearview mirror. "Hey, wake up!" He'd almost forgotten about Mike, and that was strange. Jesus, his thoughts were scattered.

Mike didn't move, so Joe tossed an empty water bottle back to wake his comrade. Mike finally sat up, clearly bewildered.

"We're almost there," Joe said. "Get your shit together."

Mike didn't look so hot but did his best to comply.

"Can't afford to get sick," Joe muttered, whether to himself or Mike, he wasn't sure. But Joe decided to squeeze in a clinic visit and ask for some antibiotics while he was on base. That would take care of whatever was ailing them. It was probably just the flu.

He almost missed the entrance, swerving into the left-turn lane at the last moment. He knew this exit like the back of his hand. How could he have almost missed it?

I'm just distracted and not feeling well, he thought.

It's just the flu, he told himself again as he flashed his ID to the guards and was waved through the gate. He veered the car toward base headquarters.

★ ★ ★

"Let's go over it again," said the Agent in Black.

Lieutenant Commander Joseph Carter wanted to bury his head in his hands, but he knew better. This agent had now been questioning him for three hours. Joe knew the drill. It could go on for several more if this asshole didn't get the answers he wanted.

Don't lose your temper, he thought. *Show respect. No matter how crappy you feel.*

And Joe was feeling increasingly crappy. He was flat-out sick. He pushed thoughts of the sickness aside and focused on his surroundings, though he did note the location of the nearest wastebasket. Just in case.

The office was small and it would have been cozy if he had been there under more pleasant circumstances. The guards outside were the only hint of threat. The problem was that Joe Carter was having a very hard time remembering what had happened two nights ago. His thoughts felt scattered, incoherent, almost as if he was drunk. Or high. Or both.

The small room and guards outside were also making him feel claustrophobic. God, his head ached, too. He wanted to put on his sunglasses, even though the blinds were closed. The glass of water on the desk sat untouched. Joe was thirsty, yes, but he didn't want to barf all over the office. Then again, maybe it would speed up this whole process.

Joe sighed. "Where do you want me to begin?"

The Agent in Black was seated on the corner of the desk—a position that allowed him to look down on the Lieutenant Commander. Joe knew all these tactics, but had never had them applied to him. His pristine record in the military spoke for itself. He'd never been in trouble and he didn't think his actions the other night were unwarranted.

"You and your friend were returning to your quarters from the bar, when...?"

"I saw what I thought was a meteor," said Joe.

"But it wasn't a meteor."

"No."

"And?"

"It landed in the middle of a field."

"Inside the base?"

"Yes."

"What did it look like, falling to the ground?"

"I just told you." Joe tried to hide his frustration. "At first, it looked like a meteor. A falling star. It had a trail. But as it came closer, we realized it was very small, and it was going to hit the ground."

"How small was it?" asked the Agent in Black for the hundredth time.

"About the size of a basketball," Joe answered tiredly.

"And you two just ran over to it?"

"Yes."

"You didn't think to report an unidentified object landing on military ground?"

"No, I...we...weren't thinking, I guess. We'd had a few beers...we were off-duty."

"Lieutenant commanders are never completely off-duty."

Joe Carter remembered that he was supposed to be on leave. "I know. It was a mistake."

"So, what did it look like?"

Joe looked longingly at the water. He lit a cigarette instead. He raised his bloodshot eyes to the Agent in Black. "It looked like a sphere, I told you. About the size of a football..." Joe trailed off. No, that wasn't right.

"A football?" The Agent in Black was right on it.

"No, that's not what I meant." Joe Carter's brain felt like jelly. He felt truly ill. He frowned. He concentrated. "A basketball. I meant it was the size of a basketball."

"You just said football. Which was it?"

"A basketball. It was round. I got my words mixed up. I'm sorry."

The Agent in Black regarded his detainee, for a detainee was exactly what Lieutenant Commander Joseph Carter was. For the moment, anyhow. The Agent in Black studied the man below him, and figured the man was either withholding information, or was coming down with something. Or hung-over, which the agent doubted. After all, Carter had been under surveillance for the last forty-three hours, ever since "The Incident."

In fact, both Lieutenant Commanders Joseph Carter and Mike Mendoza had been watched closely—followed, even, from San Diego to Seal Beach. The Agent in Black was slightly surprised that they hadn't been aware of it. At least, they hadn't given any indication of knowing that they were being tailed, other than nearly missing their freeway exit.

The agent sipped his coffee, and glanced at Carter's untouched water. "You thirsty?" he asked.

"No."

Silence.

"What did you do when you reached the fallen object?"

Carter sighed. "Like I said, we got to it and...we looked around to see where it came from. It just fell out of the sky. We didn't see any aircraft, and no, the wind wasn't blowing, and no, the thing wasn't hot, and yes, it looked like a round rock. Gray in color, but that impression might have been due to the moonlight."

While the agent watched him closely, the lieutenant commander stood and crossed over to the room's only window. The guards watched him closely, too. Carter tried to close the blinds just a little more, but couldn't seem to make the damn things work. Blast it! The light was just too damn bright.

"What happened next?" the agent calmly asked.

Frustrated, Carter gave up and faced the Agent in Black. "I...I don't remember. Wait. Yes, I bent down to touch it. I know, I know, I know I wasn't supposed to. I was just so curious, you know? So, I touched it. I'm sorry. I touched it and a piece broke off in my hand. I showed it to Mike."

"Lieutenant Commander Mendoza?"

"Yes."

"And he touched it, too?"

"Yes."

"And that's when you decided it might be time to report the incident?"

"Yes. I called my commanding officer from my cell phone." *But you dicks showed up first,* Joe thought to himself. Aloud, he said, "You know the drill from there."

The Agent in Black knew. His CREW had tracked several such "Incidents." Over the past two days, small objects had landed on various military sites worldwide. The CREW was on the spot in most locations before anyone else. Lieutenant Commanders Carter and Mendoza were two of the six in the world who'd seen the landings firsthand. As well as these two LCs, three witnesses in Mexico City and one in Istanbul were being interrogated.

There was a knock on the door.

"Excuse me." The Agent in Black left Carter with his own thoughts.

Carter and Mendoza got a glimpse of the goon in the hallway and exchanged glances before the door closed.

In the hall, the agent met with what could have been his clone. "You get anything?" he asked.

"Not much. Same story."

The Agent in Black nodded. These two unfortunate LCs knew next to nothing. Neither had top-secret clearance. Even if they had, they wouldn't have had any access to The CREW's intelligence information. "What should we do with them?"

The clone spoke. "They don't know anything."

"They've seen the crash."

The clone nodded. "True, but they aren't aware of anything else."

The Agent in Black's first priority was to contain this information. No matter what.

The clone read his mind. "Any additional attention to this could be catastrophic."

The Agent in Black nodded and considered the whole picture. These two had spotless records. Obviously, they were potential "lifers" for the Navy. Containment of these events also meant silence. The Agent in Black had the authority to lock them up. Hell, he had the authority to make them disappear, too. Few knew the agent's real name, and he liked it that way. He was known simply as the Agent in Black, a name that struck fear in those he crossed paths with. Fear was a good thing in his line of business. He and his CREW were above Top Secret; that is, they didn't officially exist. Indeed, few knew of the CREW's existence, including the president. A cabal of intelligence leaders had created the CREW, along with other shadow agencies, to clean up messes just like this one.

And it's a helluva mess, thought the Agent in Black.

But their disappearance would attract attention. Families didn't need to know, but military colleagues would wonder, even in private. Besides, both men looked ill. Additionally, both men were supposed to be on leave.

He sighed and made his first mistake. His biggest mistake. "Have them sign a confidentiality agreement. Then they can go."

The clone hid his disagreement. He would never contradict his superior. Or so he thought at the time. "I'll draw up the papers."

CHAPTER THREE

Anna Carter focused her left eye into the great telescope atop the Griffith Observatory. Her right eye, trained over the last year, phased out as she scrutinized the night sky. Her hands automatically found their way to the attached laptop, adjusting the lens.

Nothing else existed for Anna in this moment except for the view into another galaxy. She didn't feel the chilled night air, and she didn't hear the music blasting from her iPod. She connected with the dark matter, billions of miles away—and tried to shrug off the fog coming up the hills of Los Feliz.

Out of frustration, she'd kept herself away for nearly two weeks. The astronomical changes were so slight that they couldn't be tracked every day. Now, she gasped at the dark matter's miniscule structural development. Pen in hand, she took notes.

Anna knew she had it pretty good compared to most kids, but her project at the Griffith Observatory meant more to her than almost anything else. Her time was usually divided between home school, working with her father at the Los Angeles Zoo, and here at the observatory.

Recently, she'd made a few friends her own age. Her father didn't like it, she knew. He'd been particularly alarmed that one of her new friends was a boy. He constantly immersed Anna in conversations of "getting older" and making "good choices." Anna took it all in with the normal impatience of a fourteen year old. She was getting pretty good at rolling her eyes.

These thoughts flickered in and out of her concentration as she alternately entered data on the laptop and took hand notes. The dark matter she'd been tracking over the last six months was changing in both size and shape. She knew they were changes that only a handful of people on Earth would be able to discern. Few public telescopes equaled the observatory's strength.

Her stomach rumbled; this she did notice but chose to ignore it. Just a few minutes more, that was all she wanted. She didn't really need more time. Her data was recorded, but she couldn't tear her eyes away from the sky view.

A tap on the shoulder made her jump, the celestial connection suddenly severed as a hand tugged on her earphones.

"Daddy!"

Jack Carter's heart skipped a beat. Anna hardly ever called him "Daddy" anymore. Now, it was merely "Dad." He tried to relish the moment but ruined it instead. "Do you know how long you've been up here?" It wasn't a question. Her surprise changed to defense as he continued. "And why don't you answer your phone? I've been calling you."

Anna glanced down at her notes. "Sorry, Dad. I was listening to music."

Jack put his worry behind him. Let it go. He wanted peace. Sparks flew between them too often now.

He smiled and handed Anna her jacket. "Got a surprise for you."

Anna attempted a smile. What now? Popcorn and a movie? With Dad? Borrring. She said, "What's up?"

Jack ignored this irritating lingo. "Your uncle called. He's probably at the house now. I thought we'd go out. Want to tag along?"

"Uncle Joe's here?" Anna's face brightened. Her uncle was more like an older brother. Anna always loved his visits, but she seldom saw him now that he'd become a lieutenant commander. "Sure," she said, hopping down from her post.

"He's got a friend with him," Jack announced.

"That's okay."

"I've got a couple of rounds to make before heading home. You want a ride?"

They descended the short stairway to the roof. Anna glanced out at the fog and shivered. She did want a ride but... "No, thanks. I've got to synch this data. It won't take long."

Jack Carter almost insisted. If they hadn't caught that cougar, he would have. He fought the impulse. He had to let her grow up. They descended the stairs and entered the building. Anna headed for the back offices, Jack for the front door. "Okay, then. See you at home in about an hour?"

Anna forced her mind off the thickening fog. *It's just fog,* she reminded herself. She smiled brightly at her father, perhaps a little too brightly and a little too forced. "I'll be careful. I'll hold my cell in my hand." She reached up and kissed his cheek. "See you soon."

★ ★ ★

Anna let herself out of the observatory's back door and sniffed the air.

Fog covered the grounds just below the large building. She thought it was strange how the fog crept up the hills and surrounded the observatory, but never rose further. She looked around. The fog spread through the grounds, but left the grand building alone. Standing at the top of the stairs that led to the lawns she could no longer see, Anna glanced up at the clear sky above her, the stars and moon, and then down at the mist that blanketed the Los Feliz neighborhood and most of Los Angeles.

She loved the night view of the City of Angels when it was clear. It reminded her of Christmas lights, a metropolis of lights to delight anyone lucky enough to see them.

But when it was foggy like this, there was no view. Only fog. Clouds, she supposed. A layer of mist was just a few steps down. Anna felt as if she were floating in the sky on these nights. She was safe as long as she stayed up here.

She took a deep breath and took the first step down into the thick mist.

It was darker than she'd anticipated. Anna glanced at the time on her cell, then quickened her pace. The hike down to their home just above

Los Feliz seemed to take longer than normal. She should have taken the main route, but this way was shorter. The little-known trail cut the trek by almost a half-mile.

Still, it was darker than she'd anticipated. And quieter than she remembered. Anna could hear her breath. She moved silently, but her footsteps sounded loud to her. A twig snapped nearby. Just a squirrel. Right? She checked her cell phone again, this time to ensure that she had reception.

Anna had one secret that she'd kept from everyone. It was dumb, really, but she was afraid of fog. A stupid fear. She knew fog didn't change anything. Every tree, rock and path was the same, clear or foggy. Still, Anna likened this fear to swimming in the ocean. Not being able to see what was moving around underneath her scared her. It didn't mean anything. That's what she usually told herself.

This fog, however, was becoming seriously dense. She tried to shake off her growing anxiety. Anna knew that she only had about fifteen more minutes of fog, and then she would be under it and come onto the main road where there were houses.

Her heart was beating fast, though, and she was only fourteen. Anna imagined she was being followed. She stopped abruptly to listen. Nothing. She held her breath, invisible on the steep trail. At the edge of her peripheral vision, she caught another movement off to her right. Anna looked, even though she could not see.

There it was again. A little closer. Anna's brain knew it was a raccoon or perhaps a deer. But in her mind's eye, she could see long, cold, slimy arms reaching out to grab her ankle or maybe even her hair.

Arms reaching slowly though the mist.

Arms waiting for her.

Arms grabbing for her.

Despite herself, Anna yelped and took off running.

CHAPTER FOUR

Joe strode to the car and Mike hurried to keep pace.

After a total of six hours of questioning, plus the two hours driving from San Diego, he was exhausted. He and Mendoza had signed the confidentiality, top-secret papers without even reading them. He wanted to get the hell out of there, if only to have the privacy to vomit. They beat feet before the Agent in Black changed his mind.

In the car, Mike cranked up the air conditioner.

Joe forced his foot to ease up on the gas pedal until they exited the base. He drove to a local taco place and parked. He really felt like shit. Every bone and muscle in his body ached. He realized that he'd forgotten to go see a doctor and ask for antibiotics. He tried to think straight, concentrate. He took off his shades and winced as he eyed himself in the rearview mirror. He frowned at the reflection. He was pale, his lips chapped, his eyes bloodshot.

Mendoza was dozing already. Joe nudged him. "Take off your shades," he said.

Despite the warm day, Mendoza shuddered. "Why?"

"Do your eyes look like mine?" Joe asked.

Mendoza reluctantly removed his sunglasses and the two regarded one another.

"I guess so," Joe said, answering his own question. "How do you feel?"

"Like my stomach is full of worms or something, man. And I'm fuckin' tired."

"And thirsty?"

"Yeah, but I can't drink anything, or I'll vomit. Not even a beer."

"We were damned lucky to get out of there," Joe said.

"No shit."

"I mean, if you went through what I did, something big must be going on."

Mendoza nodded, then looked like he was going to puke. He opened the car door. Put his shades on again and bent over. Retched. His stomach emptied quickly.

Joe tried to think straight. Whatever they'd found the other night was big. It was important, so important that he doubted anyone knew exactly how to respond. He knew very well that he and Mendoza could have been locked up, just to keep them quiet. Joe guessed rightly that the Agent in Black and his Clone had made the least conspicuous choice by letting them go. He also felt they were being followed. Was the car bugged?

Joe held his hand low and signaled for Mendoza to stay quiet. No one watching could have seen this. "Let's try to eat," he said, motioning for Mendoza to bring his small duffel bag and cell phone. "Let's wash up, eat, and find a place to stay."

★ ★ ★

AWOL.

An hour later, Lieutenant Commanders Joseph Carter and Michael Mendoza sped up the 605 Freeway. They'd changed into civilian clothing and hotwired a nearby car. Joe knew these actions were serious offenses, but he wasn't thinking totally straight. He didn't think the Agent in Black had caught on, but one could never be too careful.

"So, why are we doing this?" Mendoza asked again.

"I think we're in trouble, either way. I don't want to be locked up. We may never get out."

"That thing from the sky. What the hell was it?"

"I don't know, but I think it's making us sick."

"Sick," Mendoza echoed.

Joe was a good driver, which was a good thing. The light traffic helped. Joe kept careful watch; he really didn't think they were being followed. Much as he hated to, though, he did zig-zag across the Los Angeles freeways for a while before entering the Los Feliz area.

"Where we going again?" Mike's voice was weak.

"My brother's."

"And why, again? Sorry, *hermano*, I can't think straight."

"We agreed that we don't want to be locked up. Something is happening."

"That meteor."

"Right."

"We fucked up by touching it."

"I suppose so."

"Are we...infected or something?"

Joe paused. "I think so." Finally, he exited the 5 Freeway. It took all of his concentration to maneuver through traffic. "I don't think we're contagious."

"Why's that?"

"Our interrogators didn't wear masks."

CHAPTER FIVE

I was making dinner when Joe arrived.

I'd made my rounds at the observatory. Around this time of year, when night came early, Goths, troublemakers, and a few gang members always frequented the place—part of my job was to work with the police to keep these punks in line.

I was a little disappointed that Carla wasn't on duty. She was a great cop. Smart, intuitive. Someday, she'd probably wind up as a detective. More than that, she was a little flirt. As I sautéed onions and garlic for my killer spaghetti, I wondered if she flashed that sexy smile for everyone or just for me. I hadn't dated much since the divorce. Being a single dad came with more responsibilities than I'd ever imagined. But I wouldn't trade raising Anna for anything.

I frowned a little. Anna was getting older. I knew she was making friends, mostly at the zoo. Some of those friends were boys. I blew a deep breath as I mixed spicy Italian sausage into the pan and checked the pot of water for the pasta. It was inevitable, I knew. Growing up. I thought about the hell I'd put my own parents through. At least I was savvy enough to keep Anna safe and in line. I hoped so.

Anyway, the sauce was simmering when I heard the knock at the door. Anna raced down the stairs of our Los Feliz home and beat me to the door. I leaned against the wall and watched as she threw the front door wide open for my brother and his friend.

Anna pulled him inside and gave him a big hug. Joe was wearing shades and staggered a little as he returned the hug. He looked hung over. That was rare, given the time of day. Evening. Anna sensed it as well, and withdrew.

Another guy held back in the entryway, waiting politely to be invited in. He was also wearing sunglasses. They must have had some party.

Joe smiled wanly. "Anna! You're taller."

Anna smiled up at his glasses. "Yep. Come on in, I want to hear everything."

I crossed the living room and gave my brother a hug. "You look horrible," I halfway joked. I glanced over his shoulder to his friend. "Oh, Mike, come on in."

Mike obliged, acting oddly, stiffly. Anna led them both to the couch. She sat next to her uncle and took off his glasses. He winced. Mike courteously removed his own. That was when I knew something was wrong.

My brother and his Navy buddy's eyes were a dark red. Not just bloodshot. I was thinking pink eye, but that wouldn't explain the gaunt faces and chapped lips. Anna jabbered about everything: a stream of information for her beloved uncle that he didn't seem to fully take in. His buddy, Mike, leaned into the couch and tried to look sociable.

I returned to my post in the hall. "You guys want a beer or something?"

"No thanks," Joe answered quickly.

Mike just shook his head.

Since when did my brother turn down a beer? I frowned.

"Anna, could you check the sauce? Make sure it's not burning. Stir it and turn it off."

Anna's energy contrasted their lethargy. "Sure! Want me to set the table? Uncle Joe, Dad made your favorite!" She didn't wait for an answer. Just bounced into the kitchen.

Joe let down his guard. He leaned back, closed his eyes and drew his thumb and forefinger to the bridge of his nose to soothe an obvious headache.

"You okay?" I asked. A stupid question.

"Man, I don't feel all that great. Hate to say it, but we're not hungry."

Mike indicated his agreement.

"Helluva time to catch a bug, on leave," I commented.

"Yeah. Listen, I hate to be a downer, but do you think we can just crash? I'm sure we'll be better in the morning."

I sighed, and accepted that sometimes things just didn't turn out as planned, or imagined. I didn't know at the time what an understatement that was. I'd been looking forward to blowing off some steam, having a few beers, talking football. Brother stuff.

Instead, I rose. "Of course. Mike can stay in the room next to you. Let me get you some water..."

"No." They said it together.

My concern deepened.

"You sure?"

"Yeah, we don't need anything, thanks." Joe seemed to have trouble concentrating. As if this was the first time he'd been there—it wasn't—he looked around the living room. "Where are the rooms?"

Puzzled, I pointed to the winding tile stairway. "Upstairs, on the right. Remember?"

"Yes, on the right," Joe echoed. He looked blankly down at his duffel bag, then reached for it. The two were definitely sick. I wondered for a brief moment whether they'd contracted some strange virus from overseas or something.

They moved slowly, methodically, toward the stairs.

"Sorry, bro." Joe's words were distant, soft.

I maintained my good-host demeanor. "No, no. You two could use a rest. Just go to bed. We'll catch up in the morning."

They were halfway up the stairs when I added, "I'll bring you some aspirin and water, just in case." They didn't seem to hear me.

Anna came back into the living room. "Table's set..." She looked around, then up at me. I could see the question mark in her mind.

"They're sick, hon," I said. "They went to bed."

"Really? I guess Uncle Joe didn't look that great. I thought he'd been partying, though."

"Listen, Anna. I want you to stay away from them."

"Dad, you know I never get sick."

"I know. But this might be different."

"What do you mean?"

I chose my words carefully, tried to hide the uncanny dread that I felt. "They might just have the flu. But they looked pretty sick to me. I don't know how they even made it here."

Anna knew me, though. We were kindred spirits, uniquely connected. "What is it?"

"I don't know. But if they're not better in the morning, I'll take them to the doctor."

Anna did a fairly good job of hiding her disappointment. "Okay."

I smiled and ruffled her hair, which she hated but still tolerated. Barely.

"We can still have dinner," I announced. "And how about a movie and some popcorn after?"

Anna rolled her eyes.

CHAPTER SIX

While Lieutenant Commanders Joseph Carter and Michael Mendoza slept, and Anna and Jack watched movies, the Agent in Black stood at the top of the watchtower at the naval base in Seal Beach. The ocean view did little to calm him. He chain-smoked and berated himself for fucking up. Fucking up in a major way.

For the last twenty years, he'd prepared for a day like this. He could hardly believe that the day had finally come. In the aftermath of his decision, all of his training appeared to amount to nothing. What had happened to protocol? To sticking to the rules, no matter what? One decision to stray from the rules could amount to inconceivable repercussions. It was his fault. The blame lay on his shoulders, and his alone.

Not the other Incidents, though. The Agent in Black's mind displayed the other Incidents on his imaginary whiteboard: a military base in Istanbul was on lockdown; there was minimal communication from the ill. Mexico City was under a quarantine. Incoming information was unclear and probably inaccurate. The Agent in Black was well aware that these were two extremely populated areas on the globe. He deduced that this was no coincidence.

Two more Incidents had been reported. China, for all its secrecy, had actually contacted Russia for information and possibly aid for "unknown extraterrestrial matter" that had been found. Nigeria had contacted the United States Secret Service in regard to a similar finding. They, in turn, handed the information over to him, the Agent in Black. *They* had followed protocol, he thought wistfully. He had not.

All of this was even above top-secret clearance. Only a handful of men were aware of the Incidents. Perhaps the Agent in Black was the only one who was thinking the unthinkable. An attack on the human race from space. Possible global pandemic illness. Probable global destruction of human life.

He stood atop the tower and watched the calm water shimmer under the peaceful moonlight and tried to think of a solution. All of these Incident sites must be contained. At any cost. He'd spoken with the Secretary of Defense this morning, requesting emergency troops to surround all known areas of contamination. He'd asked for authority to command those troops. The Secretary of Defense had a full plate, what with matters in the Middle East at the moment. The Secretary of Defense would get back to him as soon as possible.

As soon as possible?

The Agent in Black shook his head. He'd needed this authority yesterday. He glanced at his watch. He would call the President by midnight if he had to. Others didn't understand the vast possibilities. The sheer number of unknown factors was staggering. What the Agent in Black did know was that people were getting sick. Apparently, only those in direct contact with the small spheres had become ill. For now. But that could change. *Would* change. He'd bet the farm on it. He had, after all, been preparing for a moment like this for twenty years.

But one step at a time, he told himself. The Agent in Black snubbed out a cigarette with his boot. Five hours and thirty-two minutes earlier, Carter and Mendoza had parked at a Mexican fast-food joint. Two of his CREW watched them enter. Did they report the Lieutenant Commanders took their duffel bags inside? No. Did his Crew report anything before waiting an hour to enter the place to search for them? No. The Agent in Black fumed, gripped the rail, knuckles white. A vein bulged, pulsing on his left temple. He knew very well the radius that one person could travel in five hours and now thirty-four minutes. And there were two of them. What if they split up? He was not pleased.

He didn't respond to the sound of the tower door closing. He kept silent when his Clone appeared at the rail.

His Clone was uneasy. The Clone was one of the very few who understood his superior's deadly temper. He hesitated. Should he speak up or wait to be addressed?

His boss lit another cigarette. "Well?"

"Agents are en route to talk with family members."

"I was hoping for something new."

"Yes, sir. They've spoken to Mendoza's mother. They didn't cause any alarm or suspicion. She said her son was on leave, but she didn't expect him for a week. He was supposed to go to Vegas."

"Send someone...shit. Send a team to scout Vegas. Assign an emergency team to scout the city."

"Yes, sir."

"And the other? Carter? What have you got on him?"

"Just a brother. A Los Angeles park ranger. Lives at the zoo."

The Agent in Black laughed in spite of himself. "He lives at the *zoo?* How does one live at the zoo?"

"According to our records, sir, he works at the zoo and the Griffith Observatory. They reserve a bungalow on site for rangers. Two agents are trying to locate him now."

"What's the trouble?"

"He patrols the areas. Vast areas of hillside land. They will contact us as soon as they question him. Apparently, he has full custody of a teenage daughter."

The Agent in Black considered. The two missing men had to know the consequences of their actions. It could result in court-martial, to say the least. Yet, they did it anyway.

The Agent in Black's anger grew. He'd underestimated them. They wouldn't go home to their families. Vegas, Mexico, up the coast, they could be anywhere. And there was nothing he could do about it.

His righthand man waited quietly as these thoughts flew through his mind in a fury of heat. The Agent in Black had no way of knowing that Lieutenant Commander Joseph Carter's brother, Jack, also had a home in Los Feliz, as this house was not in Jack's name. It was in his ex-wife's cousin's name, and she was a rich film producer who'd taken pity on Jack during the divorce. The Los Feliz place was merely an investment for her; a large, Spanish-style home built in the 1920s that accrued equity as time passed. She'd offered it to Jack, so that he could have a home for himself and his daughter. There was no mail, nor a record of any kind that Joe Carter's brother lived there.

So the Agent in Black stood there, at the tower, and gritted his teeth. His eyes never wavered from the silver sea.

"Question the daughter, as well."

"Uh...Sir, the daughter is underage...what if this draws attention?"

"I don't give a rat's ass if it causes a little attention."

"Yes, sir. I was just thinking of the repercussions—"

The Agent in Black whirled, his face now within an inch of his Clone. "Repercussions? You don't understand the meaning of the word. I don't have to tell you what we're facing here, do I?"

The Clone shook his head ever so slightly.

"I'm telling you to talk to that girl. Get her to talk. Interview the father's co-workers. Get that team out to Vegas now, and put an APB out for both of them. Notify the fucking airlines, trains, bus stations. Christ, what the hell do I pay you for?"

The sweat on the Clone's face was the only indication he was petrified. He stood up straight. "Yes, sir."

"Find them. Find them and bring them to me. Now!"

The Clone nodded and left quickly.

CHAPTER SEVEN

I felt him behind me before I opened my eyes.

I'd been asleep...but fitfully. Now, as I lay completely still, the full—and highly unusual—realization that my brother was standing in my bedroom fully dawned on me.

My brother? Was he okay?

I snapped fully awake and sat up. "Joey?" I asked, using the name most familiar to me. Despite his military acclaim, he would always be Joey to me.

He stood in my doorway, a dark shadow among other dark shadows. It was him, too, I was sure of it. Too tall to be Mike. I could be wrong—hell, I had to be wrong—but I sensed waves of anger coming from him. Also, as my fitful sleep turned into full comprehension, something else occurred to me: my brother had been watching me sleep.

And, for some reason, growing more and more angry.

I hated saying that I put up my guard for my one and only brother, but I switched into defense mode. My gun was under my pillow, and I don't know how I could think of that, but I did.

I smiled though, as if nothing was wrong. "Hey, Joey," I said again, softening my tone. Something was very wrong. I was sure of it. "Are you all right?"

Now my brother seemed to snap awake. He blinked and shook his head a little. Then he glanced around, as if wondering what he was doing in my room. He was sweating.

I set my feet on the floor and motioned for him to sit beside me. I really didn't want to catch whatever he had, but he was my brother, after all. Blood was thicker than water, and all that.

"What the hell is wrong with you, bro?" I asked.

Joe muttered something to himself; it was a tendency he had. I couldn't understand him. He fell silent again, and I was about to speak up when he whispered, "Jack, I have to tell you something. But you can't tell anyone. It's a secret."

"I'm good with secrets," I said.

This wasn't my fun-loving, zest-for-life brother. I'd seen him sick before, and he'd always maintained a happy spirit. I was the serious brother. But Joe looked grim now. And more than a little confused.

"Not a football," he stated. "I got my words mixed up."

"What?"

"It was the shape of a basketball."

"What are you talking about?" I put a hand on his shoulder. He jerked it away.

"Don't touch me!"

"Jesus, sorry. What about a basketball? Or a football?"

He jumped up. "I said it was *not* a football!" He spat into my face. His eyes were sunken, his lips parched. The hatred in those red eyes were horrible to see. Hatred from my own brother?

I stood as well, tried to calm him. I'd never, ever seen him act like this. "Okay, bro, okay. I'm sorry."

Joe took a deep breath. Dragged his hands through his hair. He leaned on a nearby chair and took another big breath. He faced me again, struggling to stay calm.

"We found something, Jack. Mike and me."

I was motionless. I didn't want to upset him again. "What did you find, Joey?"

"It came out of the sky," he continued with a glazed expression. "And we found it. We shouldn't have touched it."

Maybe I'd watched too many horror movies, but a sense of dread came over me. I waited.

"It was beautiful, like a falling star. But that's not how *they* saw it. No. Mike and I found it, but they took it away. It's a good thing they let us go, too. Otherwise, I would have gone berserk."

Jesus, was my brother was losing his mind? Joe was level-headed; he was a lieutenant commander climbing the Navy ranks.

"I don't think we should have touched it," he continued, babbling, "and I don't think they should have taken it, either. It will make you sick."

"Joe..."

"I didn't know where to go," he said miserably. "I can't think. I could barely think during the interpretation. No. Wrong word. *Interrogation.* But I'm smart, kind of, you know? I got us out of there."

The hole in my gut was widening by the second. I crossed to the window. I expected to find the military car Joe usually drove, but the driveway was empty.

"Where's your car?"

"I don't know. It's gone. I switched it. Then we walked. So bright outside. Close the drapes."

I closed the drapes. I crossed the room in two strides. I didn't care if he got angry; I took him by the shoulders.

"What the devil are you talking about, Joe?"

My brother let out a low, guttural snarl. I wasn't sure he recognized me. I let go, backed up. He slapped himself in the face, hard, and then took another deep breath that looked painful. Next, he fell to the wooden floor, so hard that the entire house shook. He hugged himself, curled in the fetal position. When he looked up at me, I could see a little of my brother again, just a little, but I'll never forget the agony in his eyes.

"Jack! You can't let me leave here. I don't want to be locked up and I'm afraid."

Now I was afraid, too. Very afraid. But I knew I was the strong one... for now.

"You need to see a doctor," I said.

"No, no! Jack, listen. Don't you understand? They'll find me, and they will lock me up. And I'll go crazy. No, Jack, please. Keep me here. I'm AWOL."

"AWOL!" I should have figured it out. "What the hell happened?"

Instead of answering, my little brother crawled into the corner of my bedroom and would say no more. In fact, he didn't seem capable of talking.

Sweet Jesus.

I stood watching him a moment, as he rocked himself back and forth. I didn't know what to do. Then I thought of Anna. Sleeping right across from her was his sick buddy, Mike.

★ ★ ★

I grabbed my gun and house keys.

This old house had those cool, custom keys that would lock doors from both inside and out. I'd never liked them before...but now I was glad. I locked the glass doors to the tiled patio, then stepped out of the bedroom and left my brother Joe in the corner. I turned toward Anna's room and froze.

Mike was standing in the middle of the dark hall.

CHAPTER EIGHT

He didn't recognize me.

He just stood there, staring into space.

I approached cautiously. "Hey, Mike."

No response. He stood stone-still. I moved carefully around him and opened Anna's door. She was sleeping. I thanked the gods for her safety. As I turned to leave, I tripped on the large stone she used as a doorstop. I cursed silently, but it was too late.

"Dad?" Her sleepy voice carried eerily into the hall. Mike was still standing there, but now his head was cocked to one side like he'd heard something.

I faced her and put a finger to my lips. Anna saw my gun and drew her covers up tight.

"Honey, I don't want to scare you," I said softly. I slipped into her room and shut the door behind me. I sat down on her bed and kissed her forehead. She would have none of it, though.

"What's going on?" she whispered, pulling away.

I didn't know what to say. That I was afraid for my daughter because my brother and his Navy buddy seemed to be out of their minds?

"Anna," I began, keeping an eye on the closed door. Jesus, what the hell was going on? "Your uncle—and his friend—are ill. I think."

"But if they're just sick, why do you need your gun?" Anna was always observant...and right to the point.

"I'm just going to make sure you're safe."

We tensed at a scratch on the door. A slight pawing made me bristle—and caused me to squeeze my gun a little tighter. My gun? With my brother and his friend in the house? Maybe I was the one dreaming. Or the one ill. None of this made sense.

Anna backed into her bed as much as she could, her eyes wide, the color gone from her cheeks. "Daddy, what is that? Is it Uncle Joe? Is he okay?"

It wasn't Uncle Joe, I knew. And he wasn't okay. Nor was his buddy, Mike, who was going insane just like my brother. But I was the father, the protector.

"Sweetie, I think they have some rare infection—"

"From what?"

"I don't know."

I recalled my brother's words: *"I don't think we should have touched it."*

Jesus, what the hell had they touched?

"What are you going to do, Daddy?"

I thought about it. "For starters, I'm locking you in here. Don't let anyone but me in, okay?"

"You're not locking me *in!*"

"Just for five minutes, honey. I promise you. I want to get those two, ah, settled. They can't think straight, and they are agitated."

She nodded, her eyes big and round and reflecting what little ambient light was in the room. "Is Uncle Joe all right?"

"He will be." I prayed that this was true. "I'll make sure. I just need you to stay put for five minutes. I promise I'll be back."

She was almost on the verge of tears now, forcing control. "Okay."

On impulse, I handed her my gun. "Trade you for your knife?"

She took the gun in her hand, feeling its weight. She knew how to shoot; I'd taught her. I could tell she was conflicted between fear and comfort. She reached under her pillow, handed me her Bowie knife. Like father, like daughter.

Another scratch at the door. "Get behind your bed," I ordered.

She silently complied, slipping out of her covers and wedging herself between the wall and bed.

"I'll be back in less than five minutes."

Peeking over the ruffled comforter, she looked up at me. "And if you're not?"

"I will be."

★ ★ ★

It all happened at once.

As I opened the door, I shoved Mike hard across the wall, and turned to lock Anna's bedroom door. Anna, good girl, made no sound. Mike was dazed at first. Then with a rush of rage, he lurched toward me. I had his arm locked behind him before he could say "Boo." I knew, the easier I made it, the likelier it was that he would comply.

"Easy, fella," I soothed.

He fought me, then calmed down. It was a good thing he did...I had the hunting knife ready. I let up on my grip a little.

"Joe?"

"Joe is my brother. This is Jack. You came here because you are sick, remember?"

His arms dropped and I released my grip. He stumbled, caught the wall. He turned to face me. His eyes were glazed, lost. He blinked once, twice. "Jack?"

"Yes."

"I was trying to sleep. I couldn't. I don't know why I'm standing here..."

"It's okay," I said. I flipped the knife over, hid it behind my forearm. My heart was hammering hard enough to pound in my ears. Mike continued bracing himself against the wall. His eyes weren't right. They were wild. Like one of the animals at the zoo. I continued gripping the knife. "What made you sick, Mike?"

"The meteor."

"What meteor?"

"It landed...we saw it fall...we shouldn't have touched it. God, I'm thirsty. I feel so sick. I'm dying. I know it. I can feel it."

Alarm rang through me. I'm a simple man. A park ranger. A father. A good friend to many. I didn't know much about things that fell from the sky...or what they could do to a person. Unless my brother and his friend were babbling incoherently about the exact same thing, then I suspected something very alarming was happening...and it was happening to my own flesh and blood. My brother. And I hadn't a clue what to do about it—or for him.

But one thing was certain. I needed to get Mike away from my daughter's room, and secured in his own. I put a tentative hand on his shoulder. The guy was burning hot. I coaxed him back down the hall. He went willingly enough, stumbling often.

"Get some rest."

"I can't sleep. I...I can't think either."

I guided him into the room, led him to the bed. "Just relax," I said calmly. "You'll feel better in the morning."

Mike turned to face me. "You think so?"

I lied again. Some Native Americans believe it's okay to lie to protect yourself. I didn't see any fault with that logic now. "Yes, I know so."

I sat him on the bed and inched toward the door. "You just relax," I said again.

He stared at me blankly. Too blankly. There was that old joke that the lights are on but nobody's home. That was exactly what I saw in his expression. The hair on my neck stood on end, and I shivered. I shut the door, fetched the key and locked him securely within.

My sick and deranged prisoner.

⋆ ⋆ ⋆

I returned to Anna. By now, she'd worked herself into a frantic state. "Daddy, what's wrong?"

I paced inside her room, thinking fast. I had to contain these two, my brother and his friend. I didn't know how incoherent they were, but I couldn't take any chances. My first concern was Anna. Always Anna. I had to be sure she was safe.

I forced myself to calm down. I stopped next to her bed and had her climb over next to me. "Baby, you know something is wrong, right?"

"I think so."

"I think something might be very, very wrong with your uncle."

Despite her strength, and her maturity, tears sprang from her eyes. She loved her Uncle Joe.

I hugged her tight as she struggled through her emotions. I said, "I need for you to be safe, baby."

"What about you?" she said through the tears.

"I'll be okay. You know me. I'm always okay."

"But Daddy..."

"Hush, angel. I'm the father here."

Anna did hush as I ran my fingers through her hair. That always calmed her. I pulled my cell out of my pocket. Dialed.

"Brice here," came the sleepy, slightly irritated reply.

"Brice, this is Jack."

"Don't tell me you've got another wildcat."

"No. I need a favor from you."

"Carter, it better be good."

I motioned for Anna to get dressed. "Can I bring Anna over to sleep there?"

Anna looked at me like I was crazy. Maybe I was. "No! I want to stay with you."

I ignored her as Brice came fully awake. After all, I had never asked him for anything. "Here? Sure. Hey, is everything okay, Jack?"

I remembered my brother's words: *Jack, I have to tell you something. But you can't tell anyone. It's a secret.* I considered, and figured it was best to keep Brice out of it. "Everything's all right," I answered smoothly, "I just have to help out a friend, that's all. I don't want Anna to be here alone."

"You need any help, Carter? The wife is here; Anna will be fine."

Anna was dressed. I next pointed to her laptop and backpack. "No, no. I just have to leave for a while. I may not be in tomorrow. Sorry. I need to take a personal day."

"I don't think you've ever taken a day off in the last ten years," Brice's voice had a touch of concern. "Take all the time you need."

"Thanks," I replied. "See you in a few."

★ ★ ★

On the drive to Brice's place, I told Anna not to mention anything at all about her uncle and his friend visiting or being sick.

"Why?"

If I had a dime for every time Anna asked why, I'd be stinking rich. I said, "Because, darlin', you know Uncle Joe is in the military. Something happened to make him sick. Top secret, I think. *Our* secret."

"But what happened?"

"I'll tell you later. For now, can I trust you to keep this to yourself?"

"Of course," she answered, perhaps a little too easily.

"Not even your friends, okay?"

"Daddy, tell me what's wrong."

"Keep the secret. Okay?" I pressed.

"Fine."

We pulled into Brice's driveway. "Look, baby. I promise I will tell you when I know more myself. Right now, I've got to get back home and figure out how to best help Uncle Joe and his friend, Mike. And I don't want to have to worry about you."

We sat looking at each other for a minute. I thought of how much she reminded me of her mother. Smart, beautiful, inquisitive. Her mother, of course, was presently living in Portugal. Her mother, of course, had dumped me for her rich boss.

I shook my head all over again. Who the hell leaves their own daughter behind? What the hell had I been thinking? Truthfully, I had no idea my ex-wife had been selfish, although the signs had been there, I suppose. Mostly, she had never connected with Anna. Not like I had. Anna was thoroughly a Daddy's girl.

Brice's front porch light came on.

"We have to think of something to tell Brice," I said.

Anna picked up my thoughts. She did that a lot these days. "Let's just say Mom's having another meltdown."

I hated using my ex-wife as an excuse, but it was a pretty good idea. Brice wouldn't question Anna about that. He would stay out of it. Brice opened the front door and stepped outside. Not much time.

"Angel, I don't want you to worry, but there's one more thing," I said to Anna as Brice came toward the truck. Her gray eyes looked up at me. They were filled with tears. I didn't blame her. "Since Uncle Joe is in the Navy, his bosses might be worried about him, too."

She nodded, understanding. My daughter was pretty savvy.

I said, "Since Uncle Joe is family, it's important for you to not say a word about this, especially if someone comes looking for him."

"But wouldn't they help him? I mean, don't they have medicine and stuff..."

"Yes, but you have to trust me on this, Anna. I've taught you to always tell the truth. But this is different. If anyone comes to ask you questions, just say..."

"I'll just say nothing. That's not lying."

It was lying, really, but Brice was waiting patiently outside our truck now.

I put my arms around her. "Good enough, baby."

"Promise you'll help Uncle Joe. And his friend."

"I promise, darlin'."

I had no idea how hard it would be to keep that promise.

CHAPTER NINE

I paused in the driveway outside my ex-wife's family home. It was a big house. Beautiful and spacious. It was meant for love and shelter.

Not as a prison for my brother and his friend.

Jesus, had I really locked them both up?

I had. And, more importantly, I had to.

I drummed my fingers on the truck's steering wheel, thinking. I wasn't sure who to call, if anyone. My brother was obviously in trouble. AWOL, in fact. He would be court-martialed. I cared about that less than I did his health.

Something had fallen from the sky. Something had contaminated them. But what? And was I contaminated now, too? Was Anna?

"Jesus," I whispered, breathing through my mouth, recalling the rage I had seen on Mike's face as he had charged me.

Maybe they're doing better, I thought.

Maybe, but I doubted it.

I drummed my fingers on the steering wheel some more, fighting to control my own rising fear...fear and anger toward my brother for bringing this sickness into our lives, and anger at him for being such an idiot. Again. For risking my life and that of my daughter.

He wasn't thinking straight, I reminded myself. He needed help, I was his only safe haven.

I looked at the looming home before me, the familiar architecture shrouded in darkness. Somewhere in there, two men were locked up, waiting.

Maybe they were doing better now.

Maybe. But I doubted it.

I got out of the truck and headed up to the house.

★ ★ ★

They were, of course, far from better.

I found both my brother and Mike pawing at their bedroom doors. Scratching like animals. I didn't know who to deal with first. They were both, obviously, getting progressively worse. For no other reason than he was closer, I chose to take care of Mike first.

My brother's friend was just coherent enough to know what a gun was, but that was about it. I'd traded back my gun for Anna's knife, telling her to keep her weapon a secret as well. I hated teaching my daughter to keep secrets.

Desperate times and all that, I thought now.

The closer I got to the door, the more the pawing seemed to increase. Jesus, was he pawing with his hands? I slipped the key in the lock, paused, collected myself...and unlocked Mike's door.

I was prepared—or thought I was.

The bastard came at me in a fit of rage, but, oddly, was moving now much more slowly. I almost hated to punch him—after all, he seemed like a likable enough guy when I'd first met him—but he left me little choice.

I swung hard, my fist landing squarely on his left temple. The force of my blow staggered him. He didn't register the pain, but I'd brought him to submission. When I showed him my gun, he wavered. His fingertips, I noticed, were torn and bloody. There was blood around the doorknob.

What the devil was going on?

Hand throbbing, I looked down and saw the cut on my knuckles. My punch had caught him in the mouth, splitting his lip and clipping a tooth. The tooth had opened the wound on my hand. Oddly, it burned like hell, but I didn't have time to worry about it.

I steered Mike down the stairs and down again to the cellar. Most old houses like these had cellars. Luckily, mine was fairly empty. There were four strong support beams though, and I handcuffed him to one. As he struggled around, I gauged his reaching circumference. I cleared away anything within his grasp. He started grunting. Yes, grunting. Good God. He waved his free hand in my direction, swinging wildly. Like a drunk in a barroom. Except he wasn't drunk and we weren't a bar. We were in my home, and something very strange was happening. A red splotch had appeared above his eye where I had hit him. He didn't seem to notice, nor care. He looked, for all intents and purposes, like a caged animal. Caged in my basement.

Lord help me. "I'm sorry, Mike."

"Commeeeer," he growled, combining the words. He could have been drunk or high.

Or possessed.

"Do you want some...water?" I asked, catching my breath and studying him. "Anything?"

For an answer, he lurched for me, seemingly forgetting he was cuffed to the post. His arm twisted painfully, but he didn't seem to notice.

"You remember Joe?" I asked. It sounded like a stupid question, but it wasn't. Mike was almost gone. I could see that. Gone where, I didn't know. Alarm raged through me.

But, amazingly, he did try to focus. "Joe?"

"Yeah. You're with Joe."

He stood still. "Sick." Now he was miserable again.

"I'm going to bring Joe down here." Perhaps being with his friend would soothe him. Then again, what the hell did I know? I was just a park ranger with a little girl.

I needed help. They needed help.

Mike was sweating now, gasping, licking his lips. I could tell he was trying to get a grip. He seemed to notice the cuffs for the first time, rattling them. "Sick," he said again, then tried to jerk the cuffs off. He pulled so hard I thought he'd broken his wrist. He didn't care. What the hell was wrong with them?

Then he lunged at me again. And again. He seemed, amazingly, to have forgotten he was tethered to the beam.

"I'll be back," I said, more to myself than him. Hell, he wasn't listening anyway.

I headed up to confront my brother.

★ ★ ★

I tried to treat Joe with more tenderness. Before unlocking the door, I called to him. "Joe?" Nothing. I tried again, raising my voice. "Joey?"

"Jack!" His tone was low. Guttural.

"Hey, Joey. I'm gonna come in, okay?" I waited again. "Back away from the door, Joey." I heard movement. He was backing away.

As I drew out the old key, something occurred to me. My brother and his friend, if anything, were acting like rabid animals. Rabies. Yes, I'd seen a few such cases as a park ranger. Horrible to watch, the creatures always had to be put down. As much as I hated to believe it, I suspected that my brother might have something similar.

There was, of course, no cure for the fast-acting rabies.

How that fit in with the meteor, I didn't know, but for now, I was going to treat my brother and his friend—as much as I hated to do so—as rabid animals.

My adrenaline was pumping when I steadied my hand enough to unlock and open the door. There he was, squatting in the center of the room, bloodied hands resting flat on the floor.

"Joey—"

I had barely gotten his name out when he bared his teeth and, quicker than Mike, charged me. He hit me before I could respond and we crashed together into the hallway wall. We fell to the floor and I found myself pummeling him. He grunted and growled. I probably did, too. Fighting my brother in the silence of the house, I thought for sure our ruckus would wake the neighbors. It was probably a good thing the walls were so thick.

I kept punching him, but he didn't back off. He scratched at my eyes. He kneed me where it counted. I doubled over on the hallway floor near the stairs. A hallway table was nearby, a table filled with Anna's geode rock collection. Many beautiful rocks were lined up, from small to big.

I tore free of my brother's grasp and picked the biggest geode. Joey was right on top of me again—and was just about to bite me when I brought the beautiful rock down on his head. Harder than I intended.

My brother dropped to the ground.

"Jesus," I whispered, gasping.

My cut along my knuckles continued to burn.

★ ★ ★

Having worked with animals (and a few drunks), I knew how hard it was to move dead weight. It was difficult to be gentle. This is my brother, I thought, as his feet thudded down the stairs. My brother who tried to *bite* me. I couldn't think of an illness that resembled these symptoms more than rabies. But I didn't yet know what I was dealing with, did I? No. Not by a long shot.

In the basement, Mike only made matters worse. I had to maneuver myself and Joe past him to the other main beam. I should've thought of that before. I should have thought of a lot of things before.

Joe was starting to come around just as I got him cuffed. I ran up to the kitchen and brought back a glass of water. I cradled my brother's head in my lap, not knowing what else to do. Water was always good, I thought.

When I poured a little into his mouth, he spat it out. He knocked the glass to the wall, shattering it. He tried to grab me again, but this time I was faster than him. His movements were slower now, closer to Mike's speed. Slow. But strong.

I backed up against the furnace, which luckily was out of their reach. I switched it off anyway. When I was done, I turned to face who were now, by law, prisoners against their will. I was their kidnapper.

Both were as close to me as their cuffs allowed. They didn't seem to notice each other. Just me. Lucky me.

I took a good look at my brother, then started up the stairs.

"Don't leave!" Joe croaked.

"Joe..."

"Please, Jack. I'll be good, I swear." He sounded like a scolded child. Still, I hesitated for a moment. Then he lunged again—and shook loose a little dust from the beams and ceiling.

I almost wept for my lost brother. I couldn't believe I had to chain up my flesh and blood in my cellar. I moved again to the stairs toward the morning light in the kitchen. I tried to block their sounds and clumsy movements from my mind. It was one of the hardest things I'd ever done. *So far.*

CHAPTER TEN

It was fortunate that Anna was a good liar. It came easily to her and, although she tried her best not to, she could look someone straight in the eye and make almost anything up.

Her ability to lie so well was something, she knew, that her Daddy wasn't exactly proud of.

So, when the Agents arrived at the zoo the next day, she was studying with Jared at a picnic table away from the main road. Anna and Jared had seldom spent a day apart from each other for the last month or so. Some people might call it puppy love, but she knew differently—and so did he. They were completely at ease together. Anna could talk to him about anything, and he never thought she was crazy.

So, when the strange men approached, Anna immediately put her guard up. Jared immediately sensed something was wrong, too.

"Who are they?" he asked as the two men in black suits approached their picnic table.

Anna smiled at Jared. "No one."

"Right," he said sarcastically.

Agent Number One, as Anna had already named him in her head, looked down at the two teens and smiled. "Are you Anna Carter?"

She frowned innocently. "Yes?"

Agent Number Two spoke. "Is your father Jack Carter?"

"Is there something wrong with him?" Anna perfectly feigned concern. She stood up and Jared stood with her.

"No, no," Number One answered mildly. Anna took Jared's hand as the two Agents sat down. "Your dad's fine. We just want to talk to you for a minute, if that's all right."

Anna maintained her frown as she and Jared sat again. "What about?"

"You have an uncle, don't you?" Number Two asked.

"Yeah. My Uncle Joe. He's in the Navy. Is he okay? Who are you?"

Both flipped open official badges and closed them quickly, but not before Anna read the acronym: CREW.

Number Two was the friendlier of the two. "We're trying to locate him. Have you seen him?"

She shook her head. "He's on leave. I think he's on vacation somewhere." She was about to add that her Uncle Joe always sent her postcards, but remembered to say as little as possible.

"Well, we're in the military, too," Number One said. "And we're trying to find your uncle. We have an important assignment for him."

"Very important," Number Two chimed in, still smiling. "Something's come up and the Navy feels your uncle would be the best man for the job. It would really help his career if we could talk to him."

"Really? Like top-secret stuff?" Anna didn't let a hint of anxiety show. She was on stage, after all.

The Agents locked eyes behind their shades, communicating something Anna didn't understand. Did they believe her? Jared sat quietly next to her. Only he knew how Anna's hand was beginning to sweat.

"Something like that," Number One answered. "The problem is, we don't know where he went. We thought you or your father might know."

"Wow. I'd hate for him to miss something big," Anna said, excited. "You should ask my dad. Want me to call him?" She reached for her cell.

Number One stayed her hand. She was pretty good, he thought. She might be telling the truth. Anna, of course, had no way of knowing that her father was being questioned right now, too. The CREW had timed their visits so father and daughter wouldn't have a chance to talk beforehand.

"You don't need to call him," Number One added. "We've already put a call into him." Number One gazed at the zoo animals and visitors for a moment.

Anna didn't dare look at Jared. She knew he was totally confused. And she couldn't risk any conversation with him. Not until these two CREW agents left. Even then, she wasn't sure what she would tell her friend. She didn't like keeping secrets from Jared. But this was really important. She also didn't want anyone to take her Uncle Joe. Especially now that she saw these two Agents. They were being untruthful to her. She could feel it. She didn't feel bad about deceiving them. Not one bit.

"Gosh," she said.

"Yes, it's a shame we can't reach him," Number Two declared. Number One nodded in agreement. "If only we knew where he was, I'm sure he would jump at this opportunity."

"Chance of a lifetime," Number One sighed. "Maybe there's a place he likes to go to get away? An old cabin, or maybe he likes to fish?"

"Hmm," Anna tried to think of the least helpful information for these guys. "I know he used to go to Mexico, but not anymore. He would take me to SeaWorld sometimes."

Neither Agent commented on this. Instead, Number Two changed the subject. "You're home-schooled, Miss Carter?"

"Y-yes," Anna wasn't expecting this. How did they know?

"And you live here? With your dad, right? Do you live here all the time, or do you stay somewhere else?"

Jared could feel the electricity pulsing from her hand to his. He'd waited patiently until now, but he could feel she was becoming upset. "Hey, she already answered your questions. Why do you want to know where she lives? Don't you need some kind of permission? I mean, we're minors and all that."

Number One's smile fell away for an instant as he scrutinized the boy. It was only a second, but both Anna and Jared caught the deadly gaze.

"Well, aren't you the clever one?" Number Two asked rhetorically. He suddenly didn't sound very nice. The two Agents in Black stood.

"My apologies," said Number One. "I'm sorry we bothered you. We didn't mean to impose or make you uncomfortable."

Anna gave Jared a dirty look as Number One reached into his coat and pulled out a card. Anna took it. "Have your father contact us, by all means. We're just trying to help your uncle." He smiled easily.

"Sure," Anna said.

"If you do talk to your uncle, would you ask him to call us?"

"Sure," she said again.

"Thank you for your time. And have a great day."

★ ★ ★

"What do you think?" asked agent Number One.

Agent Number Two regarded a couple of giraffes in their limited domain. The smiles were gone now.

"Either she's a very good liar, or she doesn't know anything."

"I agree on both counts."

"Either way, we have nothing new. That won't please the Boss."

"I know."

They walked in silence, heading toward the exit. They'd checked out the Carter's small bungalow prior to talking with Miss Carter. Nothing there, either. Carter and his daughter lived in a very spartan way. Almost no belongings. Maybe their other place at the observatory was more homey. But he was informed that they spent more time sleeping at the zoo bungalow than at the observatory. It was a strange way to live, indeed.

"Well, we can always hope," Agent Number One surmised.

"Hope for what?"

"That her father can't lie as well."

★ ★ ★

The Agents in Black strolled away as casually as they'd come. Anna and Jared watched them go.

Jared whistled. "What was that all about?"

Anna just shook her head.

"You should call your dad," said Jared.

Should she? Anna knew her father was trying to help Uncle Joe and his friend. She didn't want to interrupt that. And she felt she'd done a pretty good job with these men.

"Anna." Jared brought her back from her thoughts. "What's going on?"

She closed her eyes. She'd seen her father do this when he had a decision to make, and she'd picked up on his technique through intuition. She held her eyes closed and focused within. She weighed which felt better inside: Telling Jared or not telling Jared.

After a moment, she looked into Jared's eyes and started talking.

CHAPTER ELEVEN

It was noon when I arrived at the observatory.

I wasn't officially on duty, but I wanted to see Carla, who was sometimes assigned to the observatory. The thing about Carla was that we connected on a different level than the other cops I came in contact with. That, and she was damn cute. Mostly, I thought to myself, I trusted her. Considered her a friend, in fact. Perhaps even more than a friend, but that might just have been my imagination.

She was also fun to be with, and she respected me as a single father. I tried to keep our conversations light, but lately, I'd confided in her about Anna growing up. Carla knew Anna, too. Anna came with me on my routes several times a week, and spent a lot of time at the observatory. She liked Anna.

I hadn't really been involved with anyone since the divorce, mostly because my trust in women in general had deteriorated since parting ways with my ex-wife.

But Carla...Carla was different. I hoped.

I spotted her patrol car near the main parking lot. I had to admit, my heart skipped a beat. I also looked at myself in the rearview mirror. Yeah, I looked like shit. No surprise there. Not after the night I'd had. Anyway, there was nothing I could do now but try to hastily flatten my wayward hair.

That was what I was doing when I saw her patrol car door open. Oops, she'd been inside the whole time, undoubtedly watching me make a fool of myself. She stepped out as I got out of my vehicle. We instinctively headed for a quiet spot in the parking lot overlooking the northwestern hills, where I could see the HOLLYWOOD sign in the not-too-far distance.

As we leaned on the wooden rail, she looked over at me and said, "You look like crap."

"Can't say the same for you."

"Why, Mr. Ranger, if I didn't know better, I would think you just gave me a compliment."

"It's been known to happen," I said. "Once or twice."

She was about to laugh, but didn't. Instead, she looked at me sideways, squinting. Cops—good cops, anyway—often know when something is wrong. They've learned to pick up on just about anything that might save their lives, honing their sixth senses to a fine edge. Like I said, the good cops. And Carla was a damn fine cop. Then again, I might have been a little biased.

After a moment, she said, "Something's wrong, but it's not Anna."

I blinked. She was good, but I didn't know she was *that* good. "How do you know?"

"You've never had a problem talking to me about her."

I nodded. She waited. Like I said, she was good. A couple wandered by, holding not-very-discreet brown paper bags. We ignored them for now, although I made a mental note to find them later and flush them out of the park.

At the moment, I was trying to decide whether I knew Carla well enough to tell her what I'd done. That is: I was holding my deranged brother and his friend prisoner. Mostly, I wanted to know if Carla had any special access to what little my brother had told me about finding some extraterrestrial rock (the size of a basketball, not a football) and their subsequent illness.

I turned to face her. Her expression was serious; she knew it was something bad. Her eyes belied trust. Yeah, I could confide in her.

And so, I told her everything. Or as much as I knew. That my younger brother and his friend were sick, that they were losing their minds fast. That both were AWOL and presently chained to the beams in my basement.

When I mentioned the basement part, her mouth dropped open. Admittedly, hearing it come out of my mouth made it seem pretty bad. When I was done, it was my turn to wait. Not surprisingly, I was sweating.

Finally, she said, "Why hasn't the military come to your house? I mean, surely they're trying to find your brother."

"Well, the house isn't in my name. Actually, few people know I have that house."

"What about Anna? Is she safe?"

"She's at the zoo studying. She's not to leave there without Brice or myself."

"Call to make sure."

"I will...but Carla, what do you think of all this?"

Again, she hesitated. "It's, well, pretty weird, Carter."

"I know."

"It's almost unbelievable."

"You don't believe me?"

"I didn't say that."

"You implied. Anyway, it's all true, and I don't know what the hell to do about it." I looked to her for some kind of acknowledgment, approval, anything—but she was looking over my shoulder, frowning.

"I'm beginning to believe you," she said.

"What do you mean?"

"We've got company."

I turned and saw them. Two men, both dressed in black suits and wearing shades. They'd spotted us somehow, and were headed our way. I said to Carla, "What are the chances they're here to see the observatory?"

"About as good as your chances of not landing in jail. They look like trouble."

"They look like clowns," I said.

"Which can be the worst kind of trouble."

They ambled over to us, looking around casually. We were alone in the parking lot. Lucky us. Both were wearing shoulder harnesses. I knew this by the way they held their left arms away from their bodies. The pistols were under their left arms. They needed only to reach inside their jackets with their right hands and withdraw.

"Both are packing," I said to Carla.

She nodded slightly. "No shit."

They appeared identical except for their hair. One blond, one dark. As they approached, the blond one nodded and said, "Good afternoon."

"They're both wearing black suits," I said to Carla.

"I think it's supposed to intimidate us," said Carla.

"Do you feel intimidated?" I asked her.

"I might have just wet myself," she said.

I grinned. The two men in black didn't grin. The dark-haired one shifted slightly, opening his jacket a little so that I could see his weapon.

"We all have guns here," I said. "You can close your jacket, cowboy."

The tension was probably a little higher than the two guys had intended. The first guy, the blond guy, turned his head slightly to his friend and shook it once. The second guy relaxed a little, settling in next to him.

Blondie said, "You Jack Carter?"

"A helluva guess," I said.

"Perhaps we could speak in private, Mr. Carter."

"How about some ID, boys?" I said.

They both flashed their badges. Office of Naval Intelligence. I studied the badge closest to me, and said, "What can I do for you, Agent Johnson?"

"We're trying to locate your brother, Lieutenant Commander Joseph Carter. Have you seen him?"

"No," I lied. "Is there a problem?"

"He's on leave, and we thought you might know his whereabouts."

"If he's on leave, he could be anywhere. Sometimes he visits me, but not all the time. You don't know his location? I mean, aren't you supposed to keep tabs on that sort of thing?"

They hesitated. Then Johnson said, "Normally, we do. But your brother's gone…missing, and we think he might be in trouble. He's ill. He may not be thinking straight."

Understatement of the year, I thought.

"Mr. Carter," Johnson said from behind his cool black shades, "we understand you're very close to your brother. He may have come in contact with a very rare virus. It tends to...alter the imagination. He may be delusional. Others have been infected, and have been cured."

Lies mixed with truth, I thought to myself. He was sick, but did they really have a cure?

The second agent said, "We're certain you'd like your brother to be healthy? It's very serious. Without treatment, he could die."

I was about to respond when Carla spoke up. "He's already told you he doesn't know where his brother is."

They ignored her. Agent Johnson said, "Jack, we understand your need to protect your brother. Family and all that. We get it. But your brother is Navy property. We would hate to see him dishonorably discharged. You wouldn't want that either, would you?"

"We're only here to help," the second agent chimed in.

I was about to do it. Maybe they were right. It certainly made more sense for my brother and his friend to have contracted some rare infection than their story about the damn space rock. If my gut wasn't screaming otherwise, I just might have.

Except...I always listen to my gut.

"I wish I could help you, boys." In a sense, this was true. But I couldn't. Yes, Joe was my brother. And, no, I wasn't going to sell him out, even if he was sick.

They're not going to help, I suddenly thought. And it wasn't so much a thought as a knowing. *No, they're going to make them disappear.*

"Well, that's a shame, Mr. Carter," Agent Johnson concluded. "If we don't find your brother and his buddy, this will develop into a criminal investigation." For the first time, he took off his sunglasses. He polished them and took in the magnificent view. "We'd hate to waste valuable government time and money watching your every move."

"I can't stop you from that," I said.

Johnson faced me. "That includes your family, including your daughter, Anna. She seems like a fine young lady."

"That's harassment," said Carla, stepping forward. "I'd like your badge numbers, please."

Johnson chuckled. He took out a card and pushed it into my hand. "If you do see your brother, or hear from him, it would be much easier for everyone involved if you called."

"Involved in what?" I asked.

He ignored my question, and they turned to go. I was about to call after them when Carla stopped me. "Let them go," she said.

I looked down at the card. Nothing but a phone number. No name, no military insignia. I tried not to think of conspiracy theories. "Do you believe me now?" I asked her as they stepped into their Lincoln Town Car. Black, of course.

"I believe something. One thing is certain, though, your brother is in some deep shit. You, too. And now, probably me. An accessory after the fact."

"Welcome to the club," I said.

"Thanks. We need to figure out what the hell is going on."

"We?" I said.

"Hey, we're in this together."

"Sounds romantic."

She snorted. "Mostly, we need to get your brother some help."

I nodded, my grin faltering. My poor fucking brother. Jesus, what had he gotten himself into? My crime investigations were often nature-related, or gang-related. But I still had what it took to solve mysteries. Maybe I needed Carla, maybe not. Either way, I had to look at my brother as a case. Take my emotions out of it. I also had to take care of Anna. That these clowns knew enough about me to know about her enraged me, but it didn't surprise me. I had to be as tough as they were. And smarter.

I took a deep breath, centered myself. "Okay. First things first. I want to check on Anna. For what it's worth, do you have time to do a little snooping around?"

Carla smiled, and for the first time she took my hand. "It would be a pleasure, Mr. Carter."

CHAPTER TWELVE

"I love you, too, Dad."

Anna hit "end" on her iPhone, then shoved it into her jeans pocket.

Jared looked at her expectantly. "Well?"

"I'm supposed to stay here, and later, I go home with Brice when he's off work."

"What about your uncle?"

"My dad and a lady cop friend are going to try to get more information about what's going on. I think. Honestly, he didn't say much."

"He probably didn't say much on purpose," said Jared.

Anna nodded. That seemed about right.

They were quiet. Jared knew that Anna only put on the angelic facade for her father. He knew better than most that Anna was much more independent than her dad believed or imagined. Jared, for instance, could tell by the look on his friend's face that the wheels were turning inside that pretty head of hers.

"That gives us four hours," she said.

"You mean before Brice is off?" he asked, catching up.

"Right."

"You want to do a little research yourself?" he asked.

Anna smiled. She knew Jared was a whiz when it came to computers. "Yes, and I want you to help. How do you search the Internet without being tracked?"

"It's not that hard," he replied confidently. "Easier if you have a large database, one that's accessed by more than one person."

"Not my laptop, then?"

"Right." He had an idea. "How busy are the observatory offices today?"

"Tuesday afternoon? Should be fine."

"Can you get us in? Without seeming...obvious?"

"Of course. I'll just say I'm working on my astronomy project."

"Ah, the mysterious Dark Matter." His voice took a sinister tone.

"Oh, shut up. It's *important* research. Did you know that there is ten times more dark matter out there than there is regular space? That—"

Jared held up his hand. "Save the lecture for later, Einstein. As long as we can get in there, uninterrupted." Jared suddenly thought of other uninterrupted times he'd like to have with Anna and blushed mightily. Fortunately, she didn't see. She was, to his frustration, thinking of something else. As always.

"First, I want to go home," she said.

"But your dad told you not to."

"No. He specifically said that I shouldn't come near my uncle. There's a difference. Besides, how can we research anything if we don't know what we're looking for?"

"Anna, he sounded pretty serious about that. This is no ordinary situation."

"Don't worry," she said, and patted him on the face. "I'll protect you."

What could he say? The girl he loved was in the middle of a bona fide mystery. And she'd confided in him—and only him. Jared liked that. It made him feel good. He also decided that he didn't want to let on that he was more than a little uneasy about the whole situation. At the very least, he had to act as bravely as her.

"Okay," he said, hoping he sounded as calm as she did. "We'll just pop in for a few minutes."

She smiled and nearly hugged him. "Maybe Uncle Joe and his friend won't even know we're there. You know, if they're really that sick and all."

"Remember, we have to get back and to the observatory in time to get on the computer—"

"We will. We can get down to the house within a half hour, and ten, fifteen minutes, tops, to see them. By the time we get back to the observatory we'll still have about an hour and a half on the Net."

"Glad to see that you have this worked out," said Jared, rolling his eyes.

They gathered their books and made their way to the zoo's exit, then along the small trail that led down the countryside to her home below.

CHAPTER THIRTEEN

Jared was getting a bad feeling about all of this.

He often got bad feelings about things—and more often than not, bad things happened. A friend of his at school thought Jared might be psychic. Jared thought his friend was nuts.

Still, a bad feeling was a bad feeling...and Jared's stomach was practically turning somersaults.

At the moment, he said nothing and blindly followed Anna behind the spacious back yards of some of the wealthiest homes in Los Feliz. Like Anna, Jared had grown up unconventionally. Also like Anna, he'd been home-schooled by parents who worked with animals more than they did people. He thought his parents were crazy, but loved them. Both he and Anna knew Griffith Park—and the surrounding Los Feliz, for that matter—like the backs of their hands. Anna, in particular. In fact, she might have even known the area better than him—especially since she often worked with her dad. Jared was often amazed that Anna knew not only the little-known trails some hikers used, but could follow the paths of wild animals. She knew them inside and out.

Soon, they found themselves behind Anna's own massive home—her part-time home, as she sometimes referred to it. Anna quietly unlatched the back gate and, once through, led the way quietly through the expansive back yard, past the koi pond she loved so much, and to the key hidden under the third potted plant from the door.

The house was dead quiet. Her father was off working with Carla, the cute cop that she knew her father had a crush on in kind of the same way that she knew Jared had a crush on her.

Two love birds, she thought, and nearly giggled.

That is, until she heard the moan from below.

"What was that?" whispered Jared. He was nearly on top of her.

She didn't know, and only shook her head. They continued through the big house, moving quietly. Like mountain lions, thought Anna. She loved the local population of mountain lions, and wanted to do all she could to protect them.

Think about the cats later, she admonished herself. *Good idea.*

Anna assumed that her Uncle Joe and his friend were upstairs, resting in bed, which was where she led Jared now, climbing the stairs as quietly as possible. When they reached the second floor landing, she stopped, puzzled. The hall was in disarray. Pictures were crooked, rugs were askew.

A stone was covered with blood.

Jared stepped forward. "Jesus, is that blood?"

Anna didn't know for sure. She didn't know what to think, either. She hurried down the hallway, and pushed open the door to the guest bedroom. Uncle Joe was gone, and Mike's room was empty, too.

"Where are they?" asked Jared.

Anna jumped at the sound of his voice. "I don't know."

"Maybe your dad took them to the doctor."

"Maybe," she said.

Anna checked her own bedroom. Nothing had been touched. That gave her some comfort. Her father's room seemed all right, too.

"Well, what do you want to do?" asked Jared.

Anna stood with her hands on her hips, taking in the trashed hallway, the empty rooms.

Something's wrong, she thought.

When she didn't immediately answer, Jared said, "Hey, you got anything to eat?"

"Are you kidding?"

"What can I say? I'm a growing boy."

Anna tried to push away the need for caution that she was presently feeling. The two black-suited weirdos at the zoo had freaked her out a little. And now this...this mess. And where the heck were their house guests?

"Please," whined Jared. "Anything. A Pop-Tart maybe."

She hated when Jared got all whiney. Like a kid. Anna wasn't a kid. She was almost an adult. At least, she felt like she was almost an adult. She turned to him and forced a smile. "Fine. How about leftover spaghetti? I can nuke it."

"Sounds good." He didn't mean to say it so loud. The place was like a tomb; it seemed to call for silence.

The two headed down, where Anna placed a large portion of the leftovers into the microwave and hit START. Jared liked having Anna wait on him. It almost felt like they were a real couple.

As they waited, Jared said, "So, what were you expecting to find?"

"You mean here?"

"Yeah."

"Well, I wanted to see for myself what my dad told me," she said. "I never thought my Uncle Joe could be dangerous to anyone. I'm glad my dad took them to the doctors' office."

"*If* he took them to the doctors," Jared said, for reasons he didn't entirely know.

"Of course he took them," she replied. "Just like you said upstairs. It makes sense. You have to make sense once in a while."

"Ha ha."

"Anyway, where else would they be?"

"They could be howling at the moon," Jared said lightly.

"Stop it. Besides, it's daytime."

Anna was getting paper plates out for them when Jared, on a wild whim, reached around her and tickled her. Anna squealed and faced him. "You're in big trouble now!"

She playfully pushed him as he grabbed her and held on, pulling her in close. The disorder upstairs momentarily forgotten, she lightly pushed him away and darted around the kitchen table. He chased her. Running around the table, laughing, he finally caught her and they ended up crashing to the floor. He rolled on top of her and locked her arms above her head.

"Stop!" she laughed.

"Make me."

Anna felt a rush of passion, something she'd been denying for many months now. But with him on top of her, looking at her with those big puppy eyes, well, she finally gave in to him. She was certain he was going to kiss her. She welcomed it. Wanted it. Her first kiss...

★ ★ ★

That moment, sweet and pure as it was, was suddenly broken by sounds from below. Not just sounds but...grunts and growls. Wild animals? Anna instantly knew that the noises were coming from the cellar.

The romantic moment fled as quickly as it came.

"What's that?" Jared was suddenly alert.

"I don't know," said Anna, getting up. "But it came from the cellar."

CHAPTER FOURTEEN

If I'd known Anna had gone home, and alone with Jared—a father's greatest fear; that is, a daughter alone with a love-struck teenaged boy—I never would have gone with Carla. Anna's actions set off a complex series of events that could have been avoided. But then again, maybe it was all inevitable.

Carla took me to her base station, the Sheriff's Department on Hollywood Boulevard. It was a fairly busy station on the cusp of true Hollywood, but Carla had a small cubicle of her own, where she kept track of the goings on in her jurisdiction, mainly, the observatory and its surrounding neighborhoods. Carla had a pretty sweet beat, compared to some of the other deputy sheriffs. Sure, she was required to keep tabs on the local gang and vandalism activities, break up the ritzy Los Feliz noisy parties, and she occasionally worked with crime detectives in the never-ending violence that ensconced the area. But she maintained a fairly local region. She couldn't have had it much better.

Carla inconspicuously led me to her cubicle and slipped out of her jacket. I sat in the small office chair meant for the occasional witness or colleague.

"Okay," she said quietly as she booted up her computer. "What do you need, specifically?"

"How about searching for an APB, for starters?"

"Your brother?" she asked, not missing a beat.

"Gee," I said. "You must be a cop."

"Shut up. What's his full name?"

"Joseph Bradford Carter." I rattled off his birthdate and residence address as she entered the search. "Can you check his friend, Mike?"

"What's his last name?" She started typing again.

"Mendoza."

Carla looked at me. "Carter, do you know how many guys named Mike Mendoza there are? It's like searching for John Smith."

I sighed. I next asked her to check any alerts or bulletins that might be coming across her desk. It took only a few clicks before she started nodding. "Bingo. There's a warning about scattered illnesses in the military. Quote: 'Yellow alert: soldiers displaying flu-like symptoms. If found, keep distance and contact local military base. Medics will be dispatched to remove and retain any affected persons.' Huh."

"Flu-like sounds about right," I said.

"And keeping a distance."

I nodded and felt sick to my stomach all over again. God, what had my poor brother gotten himself involved with?

Carla announced a discovery. "Here's your APB." She clicked a few buttons and picked up the freshly printed pages from a printer next to her desk. "The APB is not only for your brother but his friend Mike, too."

She handed the pages to me. "AWOL," it read, followed by another acronym: "A&D." Which meant, of course, "Armed and Dangerous."

I stood, hardly believing what I was seeing. Armed and dangerous meant, of course, that officers could shoot at will. "I need to see him—"

Carla wisely grabbed my hand and pulled me down. "Quiet, Jack." She was right, of course. This was the last place to make a scene.

My head pounded. Worse, a wave of dizziness threatened to overtake me. I took in some air, and focused my breathing. What should have been a nice visit with my brother had spiraled completely and totally out of control. Into something unimaginable. An APB for his arrest? Armed and dangerous? AWOL?

"I don't know what to do," I heard myself say, and it might have been the first time I'd admitted something like that in a long time. I was good at my job. Busting up gang activity, drug activity and handling wild animals in my parks seemed to be right up my alley. Dealing with this...not so much.

"I don't either," said Carla. "But let's get out of here and figure something out."

I couldn't have agreed more.

CHAPTER FIFTEEN

Anna and Jared tiptoed toward the cellar, ears attuned to the noises on the other side of the door, neither hardly daring to breathe. In fact, for both of them, making noise of any type suddenly seemed like a very bad idea.

Had a wild animal found its way into their basement? Anna wondered. Not unheard of, especially since their house backed up to the looming hill. She listened hard, but whatever had made the sound had fallen silent.

As she listened, her ear pressed against the door, she considered calling her dad. But then that would mean admitting she had come home, directly disobeying him, and she hated disappointing him.

So, for now, she waited and listened, with Jared pressing close to her. Maybe a little too close. And he was smelling kind of sweaty. She wrinkled her nose and pressed her ear harder against the wooden door, listening. The house itself seemed to be waiting, very still, as if preparing for a storm. Then again, her dad always told her she had an overactive imagination. Anyway, whatever had made the sound seemed be—

Wait, there it came again.

It was a grunt. A human grunt. Worse yet, it sounded like it could have been from...

"It's my uncle," she declared.

"Wait, what?" whispered Jared.

She reached for the cellar doorknob. "Uncle Joe. I know it's him."

"What are you doing?"

"I have to see. He won't hurt me. He would never hurt me."

Jared moved between Anna and the door, still whispering. "That didn't sound like anything close to normal. You should wait for your dad."

"What, so he can forbid me to see what's going on? Whatever it is, I can handle it."

Jared understood her well enough to know her stubborn streak, and tried to be noble. After all, Jared would have done anything for Anna... even go down first into a creepy basement filled with strange and guttural but human noises.

He said, "At least let me go first. Oh, and get a kitchen knife." He raised a hand in peace at her protest. "Just in case, Anna. Maybe it's not your uncle, or maybe he's in trouble. Either way, we're stupid to not have a weapon."

Anna crossed to the counter, still tiptoeing, and retrieved the largest knife she could find. "Don't you dare hurt my uncle. Maybe I should go first."

"Let's go together. Side by side."

It didn't help that the door *creaked* open. They both jumped at the sound; indeed, the creaking seemed to reawaken the groans from below, too. Anna always hated the fact that the chain-pull for the light was at the bottom of the stairs. She hated it even more now.

Who the hell puts the light pull at the bottom of the stairs? she thought for the hundredth time.

And so they descended the shadowy stairs, afraid, touching shoulders, and very nearly holding hands. Only the ambient light from the kitchen above lit their way.

Halfway down the stairs, the shadows of two figures stopped the teenagers dead in their tracks. Now, in the faint light, Anna could see, amazingly, astonishingly, that the figures were her uncle and his friend.

"Oh, my God!" she said and, to Jared's surprise, hurried down the steps to the dangling light chain-pull below.

Anna hadn't taken the time to think of what she might find down here, but she sure as hell wasn't expecting the horror waiting for her.

"Holy shit!" said Jared behind her when the light splashed across the square-shaped room made of brick and sporting various support beams.

And secured to two such beams was, to her utter shock, her Uncle Joe and his friend Mike. Both recoiled from the light, trying to shield their eyes, and neither showed any signs of recognizing her. Mostly, they looked horribly ill with skin that was a deathly gray, and vomit and foam dripping from their mouths and onto their clothing. Although shielding their eyes from the single bulbs, Anna noticed two things about their eyes: they were blood red...and angry.

So angry.

Additionally, both were handcuffed, which meant her dad had something to do with it. She was beginning to see why her didn't want her coming back alone.

Yeah, she got it now.

"Uncle Joe!" Despite her fear, Anna took a step toward him. He cocked his head. Listened for a second, then bared his teeth and lunged. Anna screamed and jumped back. If Jared hadn't held her up, she would have fallen.

The chained men regarded the young pair and yanked on their handcuffs harder, the metal cutting into their wrists. Their eyes...so red, so filled with hate.

Not hate, she thought. *They're sick. Just sick...*

"Anna," said Jared behind her, his voice barely above a whisper, "we've got to get out of here."

"No!" she said loudly, tearing free of his grasp. "We've got to do something. Look at them!"

"Oh, I am," said Jared softly. He didn't know Anna's uncle or this other guy, and right now he didn't care if Lady Gaga was chained only a few feet away. "Anna, you can't touch them. Let's get out of here. Now."

"We have to help them! Look, the light is hurting their eyes."

Jared grabbed her hand, tightly. "There's something wrong with them, Anna. Something bad...and if they weren't chained up...Jesus, look at how they're looking at us. They want to friggin' kill us."

"I'm not leaving."

"Yes, you are. I'll turn out the light for them, but we're getting the hell out of here and away from them." He took her hand and pulled her back toward the stairs. She resisted, but not by much. Just then, one of the men—her uncle maybe, he didn't know—literally lunged at them like a caged animal.

Jared didn't like the thought of switching off the light, but he figured it was best to leave things the way they had found them—with the lights off.

He pushed Anna ahead of him, up the stairs, then reached back. As he did so, he looked for a final time at the two men chained to the support beams. They stared at him with reddish eyes, swaying slightly...and making low, growling noises insides their throats.

No, not men, he thought, yanking off the light. *Not any more.*

The teens bolted up the stairs.

CHAPTER SIXTEEN

For the most part, I trusted my instincts. Every good cop does. And, yes, despite Carla's occasional teasing, park rangers are cops, too. Most officers feel their way through any situation, trusting their training and equipment. But mostly, they trusted their instincts.

I knew it was the right decision to send Anna to Brice's house. And, as difficult as it was, I was at peace with my decision to chain up my brother and his friend. They were out of their minds, delusional...and violent. I would deal with—and accept—the consequences of my actions. . .later.

You cuffed your brother in the basement, in the dark.

I had to, I told myself now as I pulled into the driveway of my ex-wife's fairly secluded Los Feliz home. The light was hurting their eyes...

Yes, I trusted my instincts—except for now. I turned and looked at the woman next to me. A cop, yes, but she was also a woman I was interested in. Perhaps more than interested. Why had I allowed her to come?

The answer, of course, was obvious: I hadn't so much allowed her to come as she had *insisted.* She was a force of nature in her own right and so I had relented.

Bad idea, I thought.

Then again, what was a good idea? The police would shoot first and ask questions later. For now, I needed to find medical help for him. First and foremost. Truth was, I could use the help.

I cut the engine. I'd always enjoyed the peace and quiet here. The sycamores, maples and eucalyptus, along with well-groomed gardens, provided a priceless privacy that I just couldn't get when Anna and I slept at the zoo or observatory.

Admittedly, the house now appeared ominous. It seemed taller, too, and I could almost sense the dark secret lurking inside.

"Maybe I should handle this on my own, Carla—"

"For God's sake, Carter, can it." She took my hand in hers. It was warm and gave me back a little strength.

She noticed the bright red mark on my knuckles, a wound that had only seemed to be getting worse. "What's wrong with your hand?" she asked. She leaned and looked at it a little more closely. She wrinkled her nose. "It's infected."

"It's something," I said, and gently pulled my hand away.

I didn't have time to worry about my hand. Maybe Carla could make some sense of all this where I couldn't. Although we both worked in the same field, my line of work—working within the park system—was a little more sheltered. I think a part of me wanted someone to tell me that I wasn't crazy.

So crazy, I thought. *All of this. Maybe I'm the one who's sick. Maybe I'm the one in a hospital somewhere.*

But...no such luck. Unless I was having the mother of all delusions, I was presently sitting next to the woman I cared about, outside of my ex-wife's home, where my brother and his friend were currently chained in my basement.

Jesus.

I took her hand with my good one and squeezed it, briefly reveling in the warmth. "All right, come on."

We stepped out, and as we headed up the wooden porch, I heard a door slam from within the house. No, not within. Below. It sounded suspiciously like the cellar. Carla drew her gun. I can't believe I did the same.

"My brother is in there," I reminded her.

"Nothing wrong with playing it safe, Carter."

I nodded. She was right, of course. I unlocked the front door and we eased inside, our guns held loosely in front of us.

★ ★ ★

I motioned for Carla to follow me as we crept toward the kitchen, which was where the door to the cellar was located. We had just crossed the living room, when we heard the back door slam.

Despite myself, I jumped. My instinct was to rush blindly forward. Rushing blindly forward was never smart. I reached behind me and held Carla back. She and I had to be on the same page. She was, and moving closer to me. She was a good cop, no doubt about it.

We cleared the kitchen, and then headed to the back door. It was unlocked. I went through first, gun held out before me, wondering if my brother and his friend had escaped the cuffs—and if they were waiting for us, knowing that I was thinking crazy thoughts.

I inspected some recently trampled grass. Footprints and tracks were a specialty of mine. There had been two of them. One smaller than the other. A girl and a boy, if I had to guess.

Anna and a friend. Undoubtedly, she had been with that Jared boy.

I scanned the hillside above the house, but it was coming on dusk, and all was dark. The back gate, I saw, was also partially open. Had they heard us coming and run?

Maybe, but it seemed so unlike my daughter. Not only to disobey me...but to run from me.

Maybe she didn't run, I thought. Maybe she fled. In fear.

Carla was at my side. She immediately deduced the same. I was torn between going after her and checking on my brother. I decided to do both. I pulled out my cell and dialed my daughter while we re-entered the house. No answer. Shit.

Carla was right behind me as I cautiously opened the cellar door. Had my daughter been down into the cellar? Had she seen her uncle? Jesus, was her uncle even still down here?

We descended cautiously. I heard a rustling from below. Damn, the person who had designed this cellar was a lunatic. Why on God's green earth would they put the light switch at the *bottom* of the stairs?

I reached back briefly for Carla. She caught my hand and squeezed my fingers. My gesture was small but it spoke volumes: be prepared for anything. Her reassuring squeeze told me that she was.

At the bottom of the stairs, I found the hanging chain and switched on the light—a chain that I was certain had been swaying. A draft? Or had Anna and her friend been down here?

Either way, the flood of yellow illuminated the captives. That I would think of my own flesh and blood as a "captive' was almost enough to make me weep. What had I become?

My brother and his friend winced at the light, raising their hands like two ghouls from a horror movie. Their eyes were redder. Their skin was pastier. They looked less and less human.

"Oh, my God," was all Carla could say. Honestly, there wasn't much more to say. I wanted desperately to go after Anna. But I didn't quite trust Carla with my brother. What if she shot him? There was no time to waste.

I knew this was a critical moment. Although Carla had wanted to help me, I suspected she wouldn't hesitate to shoot to kill if threatened—and I didn't blame her. Still, my foremost thought was for my daughter. Anna would be wild with fear after witnessing this scene just moments ago, if she had been down here.

She was down here, I thought. *Which is why she ran.*

Carla flinched as I put my hand on her shoulder. I couldn't afford for her to be trigger happy. "Carla. This is my brother."

That's when my close friend finally stated what I could not. "He's not human, Jack."

"Maybe not." I touched her again, and this time she remained calm. I stood by her as she processed the two inconceivable beings in my cellar.

"They're safe. Contained. I have to find Anna."

She stood a minute longer, taking in their conditions, calculating. I didn't have time to wait. "Come with me," I pleaded. "My daughter. I have to get to her."

Carla gave one final nod and, still pointing her gun, and backed up the stairs with me.

CHAPTER SEVENTEEN

Anna ran and ran.

Tears streaked down her face. She raced up the little-known trails through the hills, the brush scratching her face and arms.

She ran as fast as she could until she could run no more. It was a considerable distance. Jared did his best to keep up with her, but even he fell behind. Anna ran because she was terrified, but also because she was angry. How could her father chain Uncle Joey up like that? She ignored his numerous calls on her cell. Her uncle needed a doctor. Anna burst up and around the path with a new rush of anger. Her father was killing her uncle. Anna would call the police if she had to.

She finally ended up in a close-knit grove of scrub oaks. Boulders formed a nice shelter from the elements. No one knew about this place except her and now, Jared. She was thirsty from running and crying. Her hair was tangled, and her shoes were muddy from the recent rain. She didn't care. All she could think of was what to do about her uncle.

Jared found her sitting with her arms around her knees. He knelt beside her. Jared knew he didn't need to say anything; with them, sometimes words were not necessary. Still, he wished he'd brought some water, but there hadn't been any time.

Even with the horror she'd just witnessed, Anna wondered when Jared would take her hand. Whenever they were together, she always waited for him to hold her hand. And every time he did, she felt her stomach flip-flop. She took that as a good sign. Now, more than ever, she needed his comfort.

Jared was getting pretty good at sensing Anna's needs, and so he moved a little closer and put his arm around her. He took one of her hands as she leaned into him. Jared was surprised to discover that Anna was shaking.

"Hey, you okay?" he asked her gently.

"He's a monster!"

"We don't know what happened—"

She spun out of Jared's embrace and turned on him. "How could he just lock them up and leave them down there! In the dark. Without even water or blankets."

"Anna...he's your dad. One of the good guys. Something must have happened—"

"Don't tell me I'm wrong. I'm not."

"Baby," he said softly, trying out a new nickname for her, "I don't know what's right or wrong. Your dad's a good guy. One of the best."

"Well, he's got a hell of a way of showing it!"

"Remember what he said about keeping this a secret? Just hours ago, you were visited by some strange men. Dangerous men, I think. I think there's more going on here than we know. You have to trust your dad. He wouldn't do anything to purposefully hurt his own brother, or you."

When she raised her eyes to meet his, Jared's heart almost broke. She was crying softly. He reached out and took her hands again. They had never let the world get in the way of their closeness, or their rare and wonderful ability to be completely honest about everything. So he prayed she would listen to him now.

He said, "Anna, those men, if they find out where your uncle is, he could be worse off than he is now."

"I can hardly believe that."

"It could be a secret government agency. Like in the movies. They can do whatever they want, and nobody will ever find out."

"Maybe..."

"Your dad could get arrested right now. In fact, he might have been arrested already."

"No." She calmed herself a little. "He's called me a zillion times in the last half hour. If he was arrested, they would only give him one call, right?"

That seemed about right to Jared. He nodded and said, "Then call him back. If he's calling you like that, he probably knows you were home and saw your uncle. Anna, it's important that you talk to him and hear him out. Something really weird is going on. Just let him explain. That's what he wants to do because he has called you so many times."

Jared came close enough to take her into his arms. Even with the day's incredible events, Jared couldn't help but take in the sweet scent of her hair. It gave him strength.

"All right," she wiped her nose on his shirt—hell, he didn't even care. "I need to calm down."

"You need to call your dad."

She shook her head. "There's no reception up here. I'll call my dad when we get to the observatory."

Her agreement was music to Jared's ears. Holding hands, they headed up the hill.

CHAPTER EIGHTEEN

It was early afternoon when the Agent in Black slipped into the base's private medical facility. A doctor greeted him at the isolation room and handed him gloves and a surgical mask.

"He's handcuffed to the bed," the doctor stated, "but don't get too close."

The Agent in Black donned the mask and gloves. "I want privacy," he said, his voice slightly muffled.

The doctor nodded uneasily, then unlocked the patient's door.

The patient was part of the CREW, a scientist assigned to inspecting and researching the mysterious meteor. Dr. David Stetson had been briefed about the rock, but had torn his glove when handling it. He'd shown signs of infection approximately eight hours later. The Agent in Black took in the signs of illness: gray pallor, dehydration, blood-red eyes. Stetson also had bouts of confusion and rage.

He was certainly in no condition to be up and about, nor to even care for himself. The Agent in Black figured that Carter and Mendoza, whose whereabouts were still unknown, were either being cared for somewhere or, more likely, were dead.

He approached the infected man. "Dr. Stetson?"

Stetson didn't seem to hear him. Instead, he looked off to the side, absently yanking on his restraints.

The Agent in Black tried again. "David Stetson?"

The man looked up, blinked once or twice, then swallowed hard. A hint of recognition crossed over his blood-red eyes. "I guess I've done it now."

"You're under the best of care, Dr. Stetson," said the Agent in Black, although, admittedly, no one had any idea what to do with him. The man had refused food and water, and when base doctors had tried IV fluids, Stetson's condition had worsened so quickly that the IVs had been stopped. Presently, he was on the strongest antibiotics, antifungals, antivirals, anti-everything—but nothing seemed to help.

Stetson's gaze wandered to his bound wrists. "Take them off," he pleaded.

"Out of the question, doctor."

"Take them off and I'll tell you everything I know."

His interest piqued, the Agent in Black leaned in a little closer. "How about you tell me what you know, David, and then I'll see what I can do for you?"

Stetson tried to focus. Concentrating on anything seemed impossible. All kinds of thoughts wandered through his mind, including the hatred he felt for the Agent in Black, his boss. Nobody ever contradicted the Agent in Black, head of the CREW. Stetson was a true doctor and scientist. When the space rock had arrived, he wanted to take his time, study its elements, determine where it might have come from.

But, no. His orders were to find a way to destroy it. Make it disappear as quickly as possible. He'd been pressured—threatened even—if he couldn't follow this direct order.

Under protest, he'd worked faster than he knew he should. Perhaps even recklessly.

And that's when the accident happened. The tear in his equipment. He'd been infected instantly through the hole in the torn surgical glove. He knew it. Something very strange seemed to come over him.

No. It overwhelmed him. Overwhelmed his natural defenses. Within seconds, Stetson knew he was in a lot of trouble—and there wasn't a damned thing anyone could do about it.

The Boss, of course, didn't care. No one seemed to care about him. They sought only to contain him. The truth was, Stetson knew he should have been in an isolation chamber. The Boss was taking a chance being so close to him.

Unless he knows something, thought Stetson. Unless he knows exactly how the virus is transmitted.

Stetson nodded, staring at the man looming over him. The man who put him in this position. The man who knew damn well how dangerous the meteor was.

Yes, Stetson's thoughts were jumbled at best, but he knew he wanted one thing: for his Boss to come closer. And so he gathered what comprehensive thoughts he had left, and said, "I have to show you. Take me to the lab."

The Agent in Black kept his distance. His scientists didn't know much about the disease—indeed, they were working around the clock to find a cure and to stop the spread—but the one thing they did know was that it appeared to only be spread through direct physical contact. Yes, the Agent knew he was taking a risk being with the man—after all, the virus was still so very new. But the Agent had spent his career taking risks—and also taking care of problems. This was just another problem. Another job. Granted, it was one of his stranger assignments, but he was up for the task.

He said, "Tell me what you know, doctor, and then we'll talk."

Any new information helped. And with Stetson being a scientist who'd been contaminated, well, he might be able to offer a new perspective.

The man coughed drily. "You won't believe me."

"Try me," said the Agent evenly. He glanced at his watch. He had places to be—in particular, he had to find the two AWOL LCs. He had his best men working on it.

"Before I was exposed, I found..." began Dr. Stetson, but his raspy voice trailed off.

"You found what?"

Stetson knew he was going insane. His brain just wasn't working right. No, it was worse than that. Far worse. He was losing his ability to think for himself. Something else seemed to be taking hold, thinking thoughts for him. Perhaps most frightening of all was that Stetson *longed* to lose control, to give in, to let out that thing which was inside him.

To let it out—and to let it feed. Yes, feed. It was so hungry. *No, I'm so hungry. So very, very hungry.*

"What did you find, Dr. Stetson?" persisted the Agent.

The scientist dropped back onto his pillow and closed his eyes. "It's not what we think."

Except that the man spoke so softly now that the Agent in Black was forced to lean in a little closer. Against his better judgment. The Agent knew to keep his distance. Hell, his every instinct told him to incinerate the room, with Stetson in it. To destroy anyone and everyone infected with the walking plague. Still, the scientist was strapped down to the bed—and seemed so very weak.

"What's not what we think? What do you mean?"

"It's...not...what..." But the scientist could not control his words, his tongue, anything. Instead, a soft growl now passed through his cracked lips.

The Agent in Black frowned and leaned closer still. He needed to know what the scientist had found, dammit. Who better to contract the infection than a scientist? The man's firsthand glimpse into the effects of the infection could prove invaluable to stopping its spread—

But the scientist had closed his eyes, seemed to be having difficulty forming words. In fact, it appeared to the Agent that the man was now... growling?

"Jesus," said the Agent in Black and had just started to back up when the scientist's eyes flew open. The man lurched powerfully off the bed. The restraints held him, yes, but the Agent was sure he heard a sickening *rending* sound. There was a horrible, fleshy *pop* as the man's shoulders were obviously yanked out of their sockets—which gave the scientist enough leeway for his head to lash out—and to sink his teeth deep into the Agent's neck.

The Agent in Black fought the man now clamped onto his neck, never more surprised in all his life. My God, the man's shoulders had pulled out of their sockets—all to reach him.

The Agent fought and bashed his way loose, but not before Stetson had taken a good chunk from his neck. The Agent in Black stumbled back, crashing into the nearby metal table. He tore off his mask and grabbed paper towels to cover his wound. He was too shocked to do anything but stare in disbelief.

David Stetson was gone. His last fleeting, conscious thought was that he had finally given into the thing that had come over him. What that thing was, he didn't know. But it had started with the infection. Hell, it was the infection.

No, it was him.

And he felt no pain. Only hunger and rage.

Hunger and rage.

Stetson was gone, yes, but something else was in his place. Using his body as a host, so to speak. Something that was hungry and angry and powerful.

The Agent stumbled, trying to find his feet. His head was spinning. He was losing a lot of blood.

Good Christ! He fucking ate it! He fucking bit off a chunk of my goddamned neck and ate it!

He looked on in horror as the scientist's jaws snapped over and over. Blood poured down from the man's mouth. The Agent's blood.

Good God!

The violent sounds brought the doctor rushing in. He took one look at the Agent in Black—blood running down his neck—and backed off.

"What in Christ's name happened?"

The Agent in Black took one long, last look at David Stetson and stumbled out of the room, the doctor hurrying after him.

"Sir!" The doctor reached for the Agent in Black's arm only to have it brushed away. "You have to have that attended to—"

The Agent in Black wheeled around. He shoved the doctor into an empty room and closed the door. "Nobody hears about this. Do you understand? Nobody!"

"Sir, I am obligated to—"

"You're under my command!" The Agent in Black ripped more paper towels from a dispenser and pressed them hard into his open wound. The bite had missed his jugular by a half-inch. "You will treat me with everything you've got."

The doctor knew what everyone else did. Do not cross this man. "Yes, sir."

The Agent in Black thought quickly. How to hide this? He surveyed the unoccupied room. "I'll stay here, for now. You get whatever fucking medication you have. Relocate my assistant to other quarters. Then you will treat me in my office."

"But sir, you must know that..."

"Of course I know! You think I'm an idiot?"

The Agent in Black swayed a little. Yes, he knew all too well. The infection was passed through direct contact. Taking a chunk out of his neck certainly qualified as direct contact.

The doctor helped him—taking great pains to not touch any blood—to a seat. The doctor tried to remain calm. "I'll get your medication. What do you want me to say to your assistant?"

"I don't care what the hell you tell him. No, wait. Tell him I've had to go meet with someone and I'll catch up to him later. Go."

The doctor drew the curtain for privacy. He reached for the door.

"Lock it," ordered the Agent in Black.

"Yes, sir."

The Agent winced as he pressed the paper towels deep into the wound. Already his skin was flaming hot.

The infection, he thought. The infection.

He closed his eyes as the doctor went to work, and all he could think about was one thing: *to kill Stetson.*

CHAPTER NINETEEN

I tapped my fingers on the armrest of Carla's patrol car. The fog was working its way through the trees. Creeping along the grounds up to the observatory. Anna and Jared were both in the back seat behind me.

We were quiet now, but a few minutes earlier, it had been our worst argument yet. Anna had been furious. I tried to make her understand. I thought I did. I just wanted her close to me. I didn't want her out of my sight, especially after she blatantly disregarded the rules.

Now we were both calm, contemplative. Collecting ourselves, our thoughts. My own thoughts, for some reason, were a bit scattered. Harder to organize.

Must be tired, I thought.

Anna had looked like I felt. Like hell, that is. Her eyes were red from tears. Not the blood-red eyes exhibited by my brother and his possessed friend. Carla had stayed out of it altogether, bless her. Jared was afraid of me, I think. He should have been. He had tried to calm Anna, and had actually done a bang-up job.

I turned in my seat. "Look, honey, you can do your research someplace else."

"I can't do it elsewhere," she explained again. Admittedly, her words were being lost on me. I was losing my focus a bit. She said again, "Jared is the best hacker in town. He says we can't research from a laptop."

My brain turned—or tried to turn—but I couldn't think of a solution. I was a field agent, for crissakes. I worked with animals and bums and rowdy campers.

Carla said, "Your living and working quarters, both here at the observatory and at the zoo, are probably bugged by now."

I knew this, but I hadn't wanted to scare Anna any more than she was. The Los Feliz home probably wasn't bugged. In fact, I knew it wasn't. If it had been, my brother would have been long gone, probably never to be heard from again. Panic briefly gripped me. He was my brother, dammit. Not the enemy. Still, we would have to be extremely careful returning there. Undoubtedly, we were being watched, even now.

Earlier, when Anna and I had finally gotten a hold of each other, I'd headed straight up to the observatory with Carla. Anna had given it to me with both barrels blazing, demanding to know why I had locked up my brother in the basement—and in the dark, no less.

I explained why. He'd been violent. So much so that I'd feared for my safety and his. Mostly, I feared for Anna. Light seemed to bother both Mike and Joey. So, I'd left them in the dark, and felt horrible about it.

But at least they were alive, I thought.

She wanted to know why I hadn't gotten them help and I told her that I was working on that. That I had to find a doctor I could trust. That I absolutely could not let my flesh and blood fall into the hands of those blood-sucking government fiends.

She had simmered down. She knew I only had my brother's best interest at heart. Yes, I supposed I would turn him in, finally, if it meant saving his life. But right now...

Right now, I needed to know what the hell was going on.

"I know I can find something, Dad," said Anna now, and Jared nodded along, too.

I looked at the boy. "What do you need?"

"Access to the computer in the observatory."

"Fine. Promise me you and Anna won't sneak off or anything...we'll wait for you here."

The boy had actually looked relieved. "I promise."

And he and Anna dashed up to the observatory.

* * *

It was almost thirty minutes later.

I tapped my fingers on the steering wheel. A sort of irritated burning seemed to be working over my flesh. I rubbed my skin absently. Mercifully, Carla hadn't been summoned anywhere. We didn't talk. Mostly, I didn't want to talk. My brain kept replaying the scenes with my brother, the basement, the APB, and my daughter yelling at me, accusing me of doing something horrible to my brother. The space rock.

Space rock? I thought again. *Unbelievable.*

"What's wrong with your arm?" she asked.

"Nothing, why?"

"You've been rubbing it for a few minutes."

I shook my head. "I'm just worried about Anna. Do you think we should go check on them?"

"No, let's give them a few minutes longer."

"I can't imagine what they're doing."

"Kids and technology seem to go hand in hand," said Carla. "Using a computer or smart phone is hardwired into them from birth."

I pinched the bridge of my nose. My head ached. When had I last eaten? Carla was watching me closely. Too closely. Why was she looking at me like that? I felt a rare flash of irritation toward her. I don't think I had ever been irritated by Carla.

A call came through her radio. A group of kids down the hill were creating some havoc at the Greek Theater.

She looked up from the radio. "I can ignore it."

"You shouldn't."

"I want to stay with you, Jack." Her eyes said more than her words. Unable to stop myself, I suddenly leaned over and kissed her. She returned the kiss softly.

"Jack..." she whispered.

Whoa. Too much was happening. My head spun a little. From the kiss. From fatigue. Shock. Maybe all three.

"Take your call," I pulled away. "You have to. I'll take the kids."

"Take them where?"

Where, indeed? "I guess we'll have to go home. I'll leave my truck here and we'll hike down."

Carla's radio summoned her again. She spoke into her attached mic. "Ten, ninety-eight." Which, in police speak, meant she was available for the assignment.

"I'll come by later," she said.

I nodded, thought about kissing her again, and decided against it. After all, I really wasn't feeling well, and I didn't want our first kiss to get her sick, too.

Warmth spread into my heart as I watched her drive down into the mist. The feeling was, I was certain, love.

At least, I hoped it was.

★ ★ ★

Just as I headed up the steps, Anna and Jared exited the building. My daughter carried a notepad with her. It was open and filled with what appeared to be scribbled writing.

She saw me and her eyes widened. "Daddy. You won't believe—"

"Shh," I said, looking around again. "Let's head to my quarters first and talk about it." We appeared to be alone at the observatory. That, I knew, could be deceiving. *You're being paranoid,* I thought. The quarters was a one-room office near the observatory. Walking distance.

"But, there's no one—"

I lifted my finger to my lips, then patted my right hand over my left twice; it was the sign for "beware."

Anna nodded immediately. Jared, of course, blinked in confusion. My father had lost his hearing in the military, and I had learned sign language at an early age. I had passed it on to Anna, who had picked it up easily.

She signed: *All right, Daddy.*

Spoken or not, I loved when she still called me *Daddy.*

★ ★ ★

Inside our quarters, which was just a single room, complete with a mini-fridge, a bathroom, a couch and a cot, I signed again for her to keep quiet. I hoped there weren't video bugs in addition to the probable audio ones.

"How about we make dinner?" I said, then signed the word: house. I added, "I don't know about you two, but I'm starved."

Anna nodded, getting it, and Jared was smart enough to stay quiet. She said, perhaps a little excitedly, "Sounds great! I'll make some spaghetti."

"Sure," I said. "I've got a hankering for some pasta."

Anna signed: *Hankering? Really?*

Oh, shut up, I signed and winked.

I gathered my first aid kit and hunting knife. I caught Jared's attention and pointed silently to the bow and arrow hung on the wall. His eyes widened a little, but he obediently took them down.

"Just let me use the bathroom," Anna said convincingly. She was perhaps a little too good at this lying business for my liking. Anyway, she shoved her notepad and laptop into her backpack. She looked at me and signed: *Anything else?*

As I glanced around, my eyes landed on a wilderness survival book. I grabbed it. I turned on the TV, and cranked it up a notch or two louder than usual.

A few minutes later, with the TV still blaring, the three of us slipped quietly out the bathroom window and made our way down through the back trails toward home.

CHAPTER TWENTY

We were hiking through the woodlands.

Anna kept wanting to tell me about what she'd learned, but there was only so much I could focus on. For some reason, I was having trouble focusing on, well, anything. I insisted on silence. I had to.

Both Anna and I, and probably Jared, too, were accustomed to listening out in the wild. I kept my ears cocked for any sound other than the nature surrounding us. Someone following, perhaps.

Or something following us.

Why that thought occurred to me, I didn't know, but I shuddered despite the fact that my skin still felt hot. No, not hot. It felt...burned, as if I'd spent the day at Santa Monica Beach.

We continued on. I fought a sense of fatigue. I didn't get fatigued. I could generally hike these trails all day long—and often did just that, on my various patrols.

Anyway, I figured we were lucky so far to have refuge in the Los Feliz house. The place was undisturbed when we entered through the back door. I said a silent prayer of thanks to anyone listening.

We were all starved. We had spaghetti anyway, leftover spaghetti, which we feasted on upstairs in my office so as not to disturb our guests in the cellar. No, our prisoners.

No, my brother, goddammit.

"Look, Dad," Anna spoke through a mouthful of noodles while retrieving her notebook. "A lot of these space rocks—meteors—landed all over. And others are getting really sick, too."

I perused her handwritten notes as I ate. "Why didn't you just print all of this?"

Jared spoke up. "It would have been easier to track us, sir. As it was, I had to hack into another data base. I found one in Colorado."

I nodded, impressed. But it was the notes that had my attention. A dozen people were sick in China. Some in Nepal, as well. As I leafed through the pages, I learned that this infection from space rocks was a global event.

"Look here, Dad." Anna guided me to the second-to-last page of her notes. "I copied this from a blog from someone living in Nepal. This person reported that some of the sick ones are biting—and even eating—other people."

I set my fork down having suddenly lost my appetite. I did my best to decipher my daughter's scribbled handwriting:

If anyone is reading this, please help us! The infected ones are so very, very strong. They are attacking us, biting us, eating us. Those who have not escaped were eaten by our own people—by those we knew and loved. Eaten alive. If anyone can read this please...

Anna was on the verge of tears again. I wanted to hold her, except Jared did it for me. The little fucking bastard.

Calm down, I thought, surprised by the sudden flare of anger within me.

I pushed down my useless jealousy. Anyway, now I was beginning to understand the magnitude of all of this. I now knew why those agents had so desperately sought my brother and his friend.

They're eating us...

Jesus.

From her notes, I deduced that the afflicted people in Third World countries had gone through the sickness, followed by a period of feeling better. Those in Germany, Australia, and North America weren't feeling better. I chewed on that when I saw that Jared had already wolfed down his dinner.

Anna had done a good job of research, but I didn't think all of this had hit her yet. She was mainly concerned about her uncle, except how any of this wild information could help Joe, I hadn't a clue. At least, not yet.

"Would you like some more?" I asked Jared.

"Well, if it's no trouble..." I sensed his fear, and I didn't blame the kid. Hell, even I was nervous about going down into the kitchen alone—and Joe was my own goddamn brother. At least, I thought he was my brother. Eating other people? God help us. I rubbed my face. At the very least, I needed coffee. And lots of it.

"I'll get it for you," I said and stood.

"Be careful, Daddy," Anna pleaded.

"I'll be all right. I won't make a sound."

Once outside my office, I drew my gun. After all, I had another reason for going back down. I had to see my brother.

* * *

Since I knew the cellar door always creaked, I grabbed the WD-40 from the kitchen shelf and sprayed the hinges from the outside. I waited a minute or two to let it seep in, and then turned the knob.

No squeak. Score one for the good guys. I sidestepped the known creaky areas of the stairs and stopped my descent when I had my brother and his friend in sight.

They were both still there, thank God, standing there in the dark, motionless. A very deep shudder rippled through me. They did not look human standing there. They did not look normal. They looked like they were...waiting. Silently waiting.

Jesus Christ.

I could see their eyes, glowing red from even here. The meteor, I thought. Something is in them. Something not of this world.

They are so very strong...

Biting us...

Eating us...

They still hadn't noticed me there on the stairs. Apparently, noise was the key to disrupting their quiet state. I backed up the stairs again and softly closed the door.

★ ★ ★

The sun was setting. I drew the curtains closed, draping a blanket over the windows to make sure that no light leaked out. I risked lighting a small candle, which I placed on the floor between us. The truth was, I felt like shit. I needed to nap. Badly.

I never thought cold instant coffee would taste good, but it gave me the boost I needed. The caffeine cleared my head. Jared wolfed down his second serving of cold spaghetti.

Anna eyed me suspiciously. "You saw them, didn't you?"

I nodded, too weak to lie.

"Well, how are they?"

I ran a hand over my face. "About the same. They didn't see me. I was thinking they might be looking a little better, but..."

"But what?"

"Nothing." I decided not to mention the odd way they had just been standing there quietly.

Mercifully, she let it go. "Better, really?"

"Somewhat. But I don't want to get your hopes up."

"But according to the information we found, yes, some of the infected *are* getting better!"

The last few days had aged my Anna, but she still had the optimistic innocence of a hopeful teen. "Why don't we just wait and see, honey?"

"Can I go down to see him?"

"No."

"Why not? We can all go together."

"Absolutely not." I didn't want her to see her uncle like that.

She opened her mouth to protest, but I jumped in. "We're all tired, baby. We need to get some rest. In the morning, we can decide what to do next."

Jared asked, "Do you want us to set up a watch?"

"Good idea. You two sleep first. I'll wake you in a few hours."

I gave them separate blankets. They both knew better than to sleep too close together in my presence. Still, Jared held Anna's hand as they eventually drifted off.

I kept watch over them, fighting a flu bug, and trying to not grow angrier and angrier at the young man holding my daughter's hand. How dare he touch my innocent daughter? And how dare she grow up…

CHAPTER TWENTY-ONE

The Agent in Black was sitting on a comfortable sofa in his office. Granted, the place now looked more like a hospital room than an agent's field office, complete with a bed and monitoring equipment. Dr. Robert Kaplan, the unfortunate soul assigned to care for him, took his vital signs.

"How do you feel, Agent Cole? It's now been eight hours," said the doctor, using the Agent in Black's real name. He'd ordered Dr. Kaplan to call him by his name. Use of Stetson's real name had been one of the few stimuli that the infected scientist had responded to. The Agent didn't want to lose his mind, not like the others. He would use whatever responses they had, and whatever knowledge they had gleaned, to fight this.

"I'm tired but not tired."

"Would you like something to eat? Perhaps to drink? Some water?"

Cole knew that he was being studied like some parasite under the lens of a microscope. He understood that he was now a "case." A confidential case. He understood the logic of this, but he was starting not to care—it was all starting to piss him the fuck off.

"No, thank you. I'm not thirsty," said the Agent. "How are my vitals?"

Dr. Kaplan hesitated. "Everything is slowing, just a little. Your pulse is now fifty-six. BP is one-hundred over sixty."

"My temperature?"

A pause. "Ninety-five point seven."

Cole absorbed the information grimly. The body temperature was especially foreboding. He stood and looked out his window into the night. He locked his hands behind him as if standing at military ease. Dr. Kaplan's cell phone rang and he answered it. Cole couldn't hear whomever the doctor was talking with, and this irritated him further.

Dr. Kaplan ended the brief call.

"Well?" asked Cole.

"It was about Stetson."

Cole's head ached but he kept his stance. "Is he dead yet?"

"He was euthanized, as ordered, but..."

"But what?"

"He's still alive, sir."

"I don't understand."

"We don't either."

"Then do it again, goddammit!" growled the Agent in Black, now putting a hand to his bandaged neck. "Cut his fucking head off! I don't care how you do it."

Agent Cole did not know there were two guards outside and out of sight. He also did not know that Kaplan had informed the Clone of what had happened, and that he, the Agent in Black, no longer had any authority—none whatsoever.

"We tried to kill him. Twice," said Dr. Kaplan. "Stetson has had enough poison to kill two men."

Cole wheeled around. "Kill him, one way or another, goddammit."

The doctor remained calm. He knew a side effect of the infection was rage. "We've aborted further attempts to put him down."

"I gave a direct—"

The doctor held up a hand, perhaps the first time he'd ever dared to cut off his superior. "Agent Cole, we've aborted putting him down because Dr. Stetson appears to show signs of improvement."

Cole wasn't expecting this. A wave of hope washed over him. "Improving how?"

"He's coherent now. Eating and drinking normally. He's being monitored closely. We could, as you say, cut off his head. But if he can recover, perhaps you will, too. There are other reports, indications of recovery elsewhere as well, although this is extremely preliminary—"

"What other reports?" snapped Cole. "Why wasn't I given this information?"

"We don't have any paperwork," Kaplan lied. "Only verbal communication."

This stopped the Agent in Black. His thoughts were a little fuzzy right now. Could that be true? His head ached. He was thirsty, but the thought of water made him queasy at the same time.

The Agent in Black was certain he wasn't being given the whole truth. A part of him didn't blame the doctor, nor the others. Another part of him wanted to rip the smug look off the doctor's face. Literally rip it off and...

Cole swallowed and let the horrific image of him eating the man's face pass. He forced it to pass.

Too horrible, he thought. *Too goddamn horrible. What's wrong with me? Not you, not you...*

Indeed, very soon Cole would be unfit to lead...unless...God, was there hope, after all? Cole had assumed he would devolve into one of the walking nightmares that were being reported around the globe—some of whom he had seen firsthand.

I don't want to be like them, he thought. But he had accepted his fate. Accepted it, that is, until this recent bit of news about Stetson's improvement.

Dr. Kaplan studied the Agent in Black with unease. He didn't tell Cole that he'd personally read some of the intel reports. He didn't tell him that some of the afflicted in other parts of the world had not only killed but *eaten* humans. And most of all, he didn't tell him that some third-world countries reported rioting and out of control violence and murders and, of course, cannibalism. Additionally, some major military bases were under complete lockdown, with no communication at all. Forces were en route right now to try to contain many of the situations.

Or so they hoped, thought Kaplan grimly.

Kaplan withheld this information as ordered. He wanted to keep Cole as calm as possible. Kaplan wondered how long that would be.

Probably another twenty-four hours, if the Agent in Black progressed as the others did. Insanity set in at about thirty-two hours. Kaplan shuddered, wondering what it would be like to totally lose control of one's mind.

God help us all, he thought.

The news that some of the infected were showing signs of recovery did not fully hearten Dr. Kaplan. He knew, along with only a handful of men around the world, that so far, no one had been able to actually kill any of the infected victims.

Maybe they haven't tried hard enough, Kaplan thought, and stood up.

Either way, Dr. Kaplan understood that this outbreak could become a pandemic unlike anything the human race had ever seen.

As Kaplan watched Cole, he wondered if it was too late to kill the man...or was there still time?

CHAPTER TWENTY-TWO

Anna and Jared were playing checkers when they heard it...a crash from somewhere in the house. Anna and Jared both gasped.

Her father, who seemed to be coming down with a cold, was asleep in the room next to them. The sound couldn't have come from him.

"It's them," said Jared. "They're here!"

Anna yelped and scrambled over Jared and dashed into the next room, shaking her father. "Daddy! Daddy!"

* * *

I was surrounded by thick fog.

I could barely see my own feet as I wandered through a maze of trails. No matter which way I went, I wound up back in the same place. Water ponds often blocked my way. That was strange because there were no natural ponds up here. I had to be careful; I knew if I fell into one, I would drown. I was a great swimmer, but these pools of water were deadly.

I was more afraid for my daughter. She was up here somewhere, too. In danger. She had someone tracking her. I heard her labored breath as she tried to get away. From what, I didn't know. She whimpered—no, she yelled: "Daddy! Daddy!"

My eyes flew open, and I sat up so quickly that I bumped heads with Anna.

"Ow!" she said, stumbling back.

"Sorry, honey. What's wrong? What's the matter?"

I was disoriented. I had been in a forest, in the fog, searching for my daughter. God, my head hurt, and my skin felt as if it were on fire. I was in my house. No, I was in my ex's house. We were upstairs. Hiding. My brother was visiting. No, my brother was a prisoner, in the basement.

Not a nightmare after all. I was living a nightmare.

I was about to ask again what was wrong when I heard a bang from inside the house. The sound was metal against metal.

"Did you hear that, Daddy?" asked Anna, whispering.

"I did."

I threw off the blanket and stood. They were doing something more than just standing down there in a daze.

He's my brother, I thought. *Not the enemy. He's just sick.*

No, he's infected.

"I'm going to check on them," I said.

Anna headed for the door. "I'm going with you—"

"Hell, no." Adrenaline started pumping. I checked my gun and took up the knife I'd kept next to me. It was still early morning; I'd had only a couple of hours of sleep. That didn't matter. "I'll go. You and Jared stay here."

"No. I want to come. We want to come. Right, Jared?"

Jared's nod wasn't all that convincing.

"You two will stay here while I go check things out. That's an order, young lady." I caught Jared's eyes, asking for his support, his obedience. He nodded quickly.

"But Dad..."

"For God's sake, Anna, would you just listen to me for once? I don't know what I'll find down there, but until it's safe, you're going to stay here with Jared. Period."

"Maybe he's right, Anna," Jared said.

She gave him what I called her look of death, which she reserved for her moments of pure fury or disgust. And in general, just for me. She turned to me. "Please don't hurt Uncle Joe. Promise me."

I took in some air and realized I couldn't make that promise. Not to those big, innocent eyes. The truth was, I had no idea what I might find down there. "I'll do my best not to hurt them."

I headed for the door, not feeling so great myself. I had thought I could sleep off the flu I suspected I was coming down with. No such luck. Damn. And my hand, dammit. My hand wasn't getting any better either. The redness seemed to be spreading. I needed to have a doctor look at that.

No time now, I thought. *Later.*

Anna plopped down on the bed and folded her arms. She looked up at me as I paused in the doorway. "But—"

"No buts."

"Dad!"

"I'll be back in less than five minutes. But if I'm not, I want you to climb down off the patio." We were in my bedroom with its French doors and connecting patio. There was some latticework that Anna, my little tomboy, had used to climb down in the past. I turned to Jared. "Lock the door behind me."

He nodded and I tossed him the keys, which infuriated Anna even more. I didn't care. Sometimes you had to do what you had to do.

* * *

I waited until I heard the key turn, then drew my gun. I unlocked the safety and made my way carefully down the stairs and into the kitchen.

The sunny rays shining in were absurdly bright. It was a beautiful morning. It was an ugly awakening to the day.

I heard my brother calling now. "Hey!" Clank-clank. "Anybody up there? Hey!"

I listened at the cellar door to the harsh whisperings down below. My brother was in conversation with Mike. I couldn't catch the words. I tried not to let myself hope. They sounded so normal. Just two guys talking. They were not the monsters described in my daughter's research. I closed my eyes, cleared my mind. I took a deep breath and opened the door. Bright light spilled inside.

"Hey!" shouted both in unison.

I took a couple of steps down. "Joe?"

"Jack! Thank God!"

A wave of guilt as I descended down, my gun still drawn. I pulled the light chain.

"Jack!" my brother cried again. His expression was one of relief. He glanced at the gun and I slowly lowered it.

"Joey?" I didn't know what else to say. Joe and Mike just stood there, handcuffed, staring, looking confused.

"You were both so sick..." Words failed me.

"I know, Jack. We were bad off."

Mike nodded, agreeing. He wiped his face with his sleeve. "I remember," he said. "We were out of our minds. That goddamn rock..."

"How do you feel now?"

"Better," answered Joe. "Much better."

"Yeah," Mike echoed.

They did look better. Their color was back, and their eyes weren't so red. They were coherent. I reminded myself to be objective.

"Tell me exactly how you feel." Joe's eyes were bright, almost too bright. They were still a little red, from what I could see in the basement's dim light.

But my brother gave me a genuine smile. "I'm really thirsty. And hungry."

"So, you remember what happened?"

"Yeah. I was angry, confused. I'm sorry I fought with you. I was so..."

"It was like this rage seized me," Mike chimed in. "I couldn't control myself. I don't blame you. I was at your daughter's room." This was true. He knew enough that he had to address it if he was going to get out of here. "I apologize, sir. You took me into your home when I was sick. Not many people would have done that."

"I have to protect her. Myself. Maybe both of you, too. I might still have to—"

"I know, Jack," my brother said. "I probably would have done the same. You probably saved us. Has anyone been looking for us?"

"Yes. You're both wanted. By the military and local police. You're AWOL," I said. "And considered armed and dangerous."

This quieted both men. I needed to think this through. Joe did look better. Maybe too good, for what he'd been through. He saw me looking at him.

"Jack, I swear we're better." His speech was a little animated, maybe because he wanted those cuffs off. Water, food, a shower. I could understand that. But...

"Let me get you some water, and then we'll talk."

"You're not going to let us out of here?"

"Shit, Joey. I want to. You don't know how hard it was to put you down here."

"Okay, okay. Water would be great."

"I'll be right back."

I didn't want to keep Anna waiting. I rounded the corner to the stairwell and found her and Jared huddled next to each other halfway down the stairs.

"What the hell are you doing here?"

"Sorry, I just had to listen. Don't blame Jared."

I exploded. "Anna, this is no game. Get the hell upstairs. Now! Both of you!" I felt more anger than I had in quite a long time.

I grabbed the key that Jared held. Anna knew she'd pushed my limit and quickly back-pedaled up the stairs. I followed them up into my room. I could feel my cheeks flush with anger as I crossed the room without a glance at either of them and slammed the door shut. I locked it.

I shoved down the guilt of locking my daughter and her boyfriend in a room. *Desperate times call for desperate measures,* I thought wildly. I moved quickly back down the stairs. In the kitchen, I grabbed two glasses out of the dishwasher, thought about it, and then exchanged them for plastic cups. No use giving anyone a weapon.

In that moment, as I filled the red Solo cups under the faucet, my hands started shaking and I felt sick, so sick. I poured out the filled cups, watching the water swirl down the drain. The pressure of the day—my sick brother, the government agents, the yelling at my daughter—it all came crashing down on me.

I pounded my fist on the tile counter. Let the damn tears come. It wasn't as if I could stop them anyway. I turned around and faced the door that led to my imprisoned brother and another man I didn't know from Adam. What was wrong with me? I couldn't control myself. Couldn't control the emotions. Couldn't control the anger.

I knocked the cups into the sink and slid down, my back to the cabinets. I sat there in anguish, the waterworks rushing from me now. Was I going crazy myself? I had handcuffed infected people in my cellar, and had locked up my daughter with a horny fifteen-year-old boy who was crazy about her. What could be more insane?

Just a few days ago, the world had been normal. Life had been good. Balanced. I didn't know if I could handle this.

So, a pent-up volcano of misery, I sat there with my legs stuck straight out and erupted. The cork on my uncontrollable emotions popped. Emotions that I hadn't let myself feel in years, decades even, spewed out. Some hero I was. *Not.*

I wept for the loss and the horror of the infected, and I raged for those who tried to help them and then, I screamed for those who tried to kill them. I sobbed and shouted until my throat was scorched from screaming my anguish, and from eyes that felt like they had sand thrown in them. Tears salted my gritty neck for the first time in decades. I was crying so hard that the pots and pans rattled in the kitchen cabinet against my back.

And that's how Carla found me.

CHAPTER TWENTY-THREE

Carla grabbed a roll of paper towels off the counter and sat beside me, cross-legged.

I chided myself for not hearing her enter through the back door; at the same time, I didn't really care. It was Carla. Safe. A friend. She was the only friend I'd confided in. And she just waited, like friends do.

It was strange how I really didn't care that she watched me cry. I usually kept up the macho façade that men tend to muster up around women. But I was so tired that I just didn't care.

A few minutes passed and my sobbing lost steam, as if the supply of tears had been exhausted and as if the volcano inside me was quieted, except for the occasional shuddering rumble of breath. I took the paper towels from her and cleaned myself up. I gathered what rational thoughts I could and faced her. "They seem to be recovering."

"Really." No judgment, just a statement. Her eyes were concerned, but serene.

"Yeah. I'm supposed to give them some water. They didn't want water before."

"And Anna?" Carla was cool, logical.

"I locked her up in my bedroom. She disobeyed my orders to stay away from them."

Carla nodded. "So, we give them some water."

"I suppose so."

"Tell you what. Get them water...and Carter?" She took the hand that wasn't holding my gun. Her other hand turned my face toward her. "It's a lot—them, your daughter, the boyfriend, the agents—it's okay to let it out sometimes."

I nodded, and I might have fallen in love with her a little more right then and there. "Thank you."

"But let's be smart. Yes, he's your brother, but this situation is so damn unusual. Hell, it's unprecedented. All the more reason to keep our heads and our wits about us."

Thank God for Carla. She was always there when I needed her most. "Right."

She rose and gave me a hand up. I didn't mind that she was the strong one in this moment.

I again filled the red plastic cups with water. We crossed the short distance to the cellar door.

Carla drew her own gun. "It might be better if I was the heavy," she observed. "Put your gun away. I'll stay back, but I'll have you covered."

Good cop. Bad cop. She was smart.

My hands were occupied with water cups so she opened the door for me and we went down to my captives.

★ ★ ★

Joe and Mike smiled in relief when they saw me. They were a little wary of Carla, but they weren't calling the shots.

Carla was professional, fierce. "Joe, Mike. Do you mind moving back a little?"

I tried to be nice. "I'll set down the water for you."

Mike complied without hesitation. Joe looked hurt, but he submitted as well. They backed away to the far side of the beams that held them captive. I set down the cups. I backed away and moved next to Carla. "Go ahead."

Both moved forward and drained the cups in an instant.

"More?" I asked.

Joe was ravenously thirsty, I could tell. "Please."

"Go," Carla said. "I'll stay."

I returned with refilled cups. They drank. I didn't want them to overdo it, but they were seriously dehydrated. Already my brother Joey looked stronger, and so did Mike.

"Thank you." Joe's face portrayed sincere gratitude, except—dammit—except that his eyes briefly flared red. *Shit.*

"Still feeling better?" I asked. Carla was calm, collected. I was glad she was with me.

"Yeah," Joe answered.

Carla caught my attention and jerked her head up to the kitchen.

"Hang on, Joey," I said. "I'll bring you some food."

I turned my back on them and followed Carla up into the kitchen. I shut the door to the basement as Carla leaned a hip against the counter. A nice, curvy hip.

"They do look better," said Carla. "But their eyes, Carter. I don't think it's over."

"You're right," I conceded. "How about we first get Joe out? He's my brother. I know I can reason with him."

"What if there's no reasoning with him?"

"Then I'll put him back down there."

I waited for Carla to think it through. "All right," she agreed, "Let me listen. Just for perspective."

"I'll question him," I said. "Maybe he knows something else, or not. I won't know until I can talk to him."

Carla nodded and I saw the genuine concern in her eyes, and perhaps I saw something else. Love? Whatever it was, I hadn't had a woman look at me like that for a very long time. I reached out and brushed my hand along her cheek. "Thank you for coming."

Carla kissed me lightly, then hugged me tight. That hug gave me the strength I needed.

★ ★ ★

I leaned back in the patio chair and watched my brother eat the oatmeal I'd made for him. Seated a short distance away, Carla appeared relaxed. She had her cop shades on. Behind her nonchalant pose, I knew she was scrutinizing Joe's every movement. I didn't blame her.

"How is it?" I asked.

He looked from me to Carla, then back to me. He knew he was being studied like a rat in a cage. I didn't care if he knew. My brother might have contracted something freaky, and we weren't going to take any chances. Period.

He said, "Honestly? It tastes okay, but I'd rather have a steak."

"Maybe you're anemic," I said. What I didn't say was: *Maybe that goddamned space rock screwed you up.*

"Maybe." He kept eating, but without enthusiasm. I got the feeling that he was trying to please me. "So...Mike and I...we're not an isolated event?"

"No." I had briefed him on what Anna had gleaned from the internet. He had listened quietly, impassively. I had expected a different reaction from someone who had just learned that he might soon be going crazy and start eating other human beings. Instead, he took the news in stride. Too much in stride, I thought.

"Are the others getting better?"

"Some."

He looked at me. "Do you think I'm getting better?"

I did my best to hide my breaking heart. "Joey, you do look better. But your eyes..."

He shook his head excitedly. "Jack, all my senses are heightened. I can see better than before. I hear everything. There's a cat on the other side of your garden wall. A hummingbird is two houses over. Anna and Jared are talking quietly. I can't understand what they're saying, but I know you don't hear them at all. Do you?"

"No, I don't." I turned my head, slightly curious about the cat. I also turned my head because I didn't want to look at my kid brother. "How's your mind, Joey? You were delusional. You were also vicious."

"I know, and I'm sorry."

"And now? I mean, I need to know how you really *feel*." I tapped my head.

He considered my question, his eyes flashing briefly red. Eyes shouldn't look like that. And my brother shouldn't be hearing a goddamn hummingbird two houses down either.

Jesus Christ.

For a moment, I didn't think he was going to answer me. He glanced briefly at Carla and hesitated, and I suddenly understood his apprehension. He didn't feel comfortable speaking freely. Maybe if Carla hadn't been there, he would have told the truth. He might have told me about the insatiable hunger...

Might have.

Perhaps if he had, things might have turned out differently. Perhaps. I'll never know. One tiny thing like Carla's presence, which had been well-intended, might have have possibly turned the giant tide.

But she was there, and I didn't even know about the enormous tide yet, and it might not have mattered anyway.

I guess my brother was as honest as he could be. "I don't feel anger or irritation, Jack. But I do feel more alive than I ever have in my entire life. I feel really strong, too. You know? Stronger than before. It's weird."

Now I studied him. His color was back to normal. Yes, he did have a healthy glow. The only trace of illness left now was in his eyes. His red eyes. No, they weren't completely red. The whites were still white. It was his irises. Once a dark green, they were now streaked with red, as if he was wearing some crazy Halloween costume contact lenses. His eyes gave me the damn creeps. God, I really hoped he was better.

"And," he continued, "like I said. I'm really hungry. Starving. And the oatmeal just ain't doing it for me, bro."

"Do you feel like you're better? Be honest."

Again, he hesitated. He was trying, I knew that now. "I think so."

I waited. I wish now that I'd known what he was really thinking. It could have made a difference.

"The truth is," he added. "I'm not a hundred percent sure, Jack. Maybe I'll feel better if I can, you know, eat some more."

I considered what I had to say. Again, if Carla hadn't been there, I might not have been able to have the courage to say to my own brother what I was about to say. "Joe. You know I love you."

"Ditto, bro." His smile was bittersweet.

I said, "If you're really thinking straight, then I hope you understand that I think we need to give this a little more time, you know?"

"What do you mean?"

"I want you to wait this out in the cellar."

He drew a deep breath.

I tensed.

So did Carla. Her hand was resting loosely on the butt of her pistol.

Joe let out his air. "Okay, yes. I do understand. I'll go back down there. Can you just leave the light on this time? It doesn't hurt our eyes so much."

I gave his arm a squeeze. "Of course."

There didn't seem to be anything else to say. My brother looked out the kitchen window, taking in the morning blue sky as if for the last time.

★ ★ ★

In the cellar, I gave him a hug before I cuffed him again. Mike was quiet. No doubt, he was waiting for me to leave so he could talk to his cellmate.

I left the light on, as requested. I felt guilty as hell cuffing my brother down here again. But I would have felt worse if he'd hurt himself or someone I loved. I debated, and then turned and asked him, "How do you want your steak?"

His answer was immediate, and as he spoke his pupils flared brightly red. "Rare."

My brother, of course, had never ordered his steaks rare. I should know. We'd barbequed enough times together. He always ordered them, in fact, medium-well.

"Rare?" I repeated.

Next to him, Mike nodded as well, his eyes equally red.

Joe said, "Rare. Very, very rare."

CHAPTER TWENTY-FOUR

When I unlocked my bedroom door shortly thereafter, Anna practically flung herself at me, furious. It took me minutes to calm her down. When she finally agreed, she understood that I had done my best, under the circumstances, to keep her and Jared safe.

"Fine," she said, glaring at me. "But I still hate you."

"You can hate me all you want, but at least you're alive."

Anna was elated to know that her Uncle Joe was feeling much better and asking for food. Of course she wanted to see him, too.

I considered her request. "Carla's downstairs making some steaks now. I suppose you can see him when we bring down their food. But Anna, I don't want you to touch him."

"But if he's getting better—"

"Until I know for sure this isn't contagious, you're not coming into contact with him."

"But didn't you come into contact with him?"

I had, of course, and it was something I was doing my damndest to ignore. Especially considering that I was feeling worse and worse.

"Let's not talk about that now, baby."

"Uh, sir?" Jared spoke up. "Is there any more steak left? We haven't eaten yet."

"Of course," I answered. Where was my head? "Do your parents know where you are?"

He held up his phone. "They know I'm okay."

"Do they know you're here?"

He blushed a little. "No, sir. Not really. I told them I was with another friend." He looked at Anna and blushed some more, then looked at me again. "It seemed too complicated to try to explain. I'm sorry I lied."

My thoughts were getting fuzzier and fuzzier. "Don't you think you should go home? Won't they want to see you?" My voice drifted. I had lost my train of thought. What the hell was wrong with me?

"It's okay," said Jared. "They work a lot, you know, at the zoo. We hardly see each other anyway."

"Jared?"

"Yes, sir?"

"You don't have to call me sir all the time. I appreciate your respect, though. Call me Jack."

"Thank you, um, Jack."

"Let's go!" Anna was smiling now. "We're hungry and I want to see Uncle Joe!"

"All right, all right. But remember your promise. You can talk, but no touching—and don't get too close, either. Can I trust you?"

"Yes, Dad. *Geeeez!*"

★ ★ ★

The two infected men sat now, facing each other. They'd been given wet cloths to clean themselves up, toothbrushes and a comb. They'd washed their faces and felt fairly decent. Except for the hunger.

"So, you told him about the heightened senses?" Mike asked. They were alone in the basement. Their voices echoed, and sometimes they heard critters rustling around in the shadows. Rats. Joe was mildly disturbed that his stomach actually growled when he thought of the rats. They could hear footsteps above, and the sound of someone cooking in the kitchen.

"Yeah. It *is* kind of cool, don't you think?"

"Hell, yes. I feel better than I've ever felt. Like I could take on an army."

"Me, too."

They had a sort of kindred connection now, these two. Neither knew what to expect next, but whatever happened, they were in this mess together. Joe had briefed Mike on the information that Anna had found on the Internet. They understood that Anna had probably only skimmed the surface of the similar incidents happening around the world. Military communications were separate from Internet news. They knew that. It was clear to both of them that something serious was going down. What they didn't know—and what wouldn't come to light for a few days, as more about the infection was understood—was that they were in their most lucid, most intelligent stage of the illness. They, like the others who were infected, had good intentions, despite a growing appetite.

"We've got to get out of here," Joe said quietly. "My brother cares about me, but I want to get back to the base."

Mike wasn't too sure what he wanted. He understood his precarious position, protected from the Agents at the home of his friend's brother. What a miracle that was. How they hadn't been tracked down, he didn't know. He was sure it was only a matter of time. Mostly, he didn't want to be a guinea pig for the military.

"I don't know about that, man," he said. "Don't you think military prison would be worse than this? We'd be poked and prodded every way to Friday. The interrogations...Jesus. It might be better to stay low."

Joe Carter regarded his longtime friend. "Mike. I know we're better. But do you feel, uh, somehow different? Aside from the 'super power' feeling?"

Mike cocked his head to make sure no one was listening from the kitchen door upstairs. "A little. A kind of...craving."

As he spoke those words, an image came to Mendoza—an image of what he was craving most—and his stomach growled.

Perhaps it was courage that kept them from speaking truthfully. Perhaps it was self-protection. Selfishness, maybe. It didn't matter, though. They didn't need to say it out loud. They now understood one another. The cravings they felt were only quenched by their hyper-comprehensive minds.

"Yeah."

Joe Carter and Mike Mendoza, both infected 48 hours earlier, were about another 48 hours away from total insanity, but they didn't know it. They had the craving, yes, but Joe still felt love. For his brother. For his niece. It was a different kind of love. He recognized it, even through his illness.

He leaned as close as he could to his friend. "If you touch them, I will kill you."

"Even the girl?"

"Especially the girl, goddammit."

Mike nodded, hearing his friend. There was a whole world of humans aside from those in this house. For now, he said, "I promise you." His sincerity seemed genuine, and Joe accepted it.

Mike was getting to the point where he didn't care about Joe's threats. Mike was getting to the point where he didn't care much about Joe either.

Fuck him, he thought.

Joe closed his eyes and focused his mind within. Weighed the situation.

Mike waited.

Joe said, "When the time is right, we go."

Excitement bloomed on Mike's face. "All right."

"I'm not sure whether we'll go back to the base or not. You can come with me if you want, or you can go your own way. But you can't stay here."

"I understand, brother," Mike Mendoza answered truthfully. They *were* brothers now. Perhaps they were closer than blood, closer than Joe was with Jack. They were comrades with a common but unspoken goal. But Joe's gut told him he had to watch Mike. After all, Mike had been standing outside of Anna's room earlier, watching.

And waiting. And hungry. Very, very hungry.

And I'm hungry, too, Joe thought. *God help me, I'm hungry.*

CHAPTER TWENTY-FIVE

It happened quickly.

Stetson was feeling much better, and he was very smart. He knew very well that he was a prime case. He knew that he was being closely monitored. So, he calmly let them take his vital signs and carefully answered all of their questions. Yes, he had heightened senses. Yes, he now craved water and food like a normal person. He ate what they brought him, although it was not nearly enough meat for his hungry new body. He flirted with the nurse. He bonded with the new doctor, and talked about family and children and empathized with the tremendous stress that the doctor was under.

Stetson made subtle inquiries about the Agent in Black, the man he'd bitten in a fit of rage. He knew that the Agent in Black had ordered him killed, and that he, Stetson, had resisted the deadly cocktail. Stetson knew it was only a matter of time before another attempt was made on his life...one that Stetson might not ward off this time. One that might finally kill him.

The scientist in him was intrigued by the possibilities of his powerful new body. But the scientist had taken a distant back seat to the Hunger, as he now thought of it.

The overwhelming hunger...

And the need to preserve his own life.

So, when PA Cheryl Parker came in to give him his meds and take his vitals yet again, Stetson decided that now was the time to make his move.

"How are we feeling now, David?" Cheryl's voice was a combination of cheerfulness and professionalism.

"About the same," Stetson answered. "I'm hungry again."

Cheryl chuckled. "That's a good sign. Anything in particular you'd like?"

David Stetson would have liked nothing better than fresh meat. Human meat. It didn't seem strange to him now. It was just the way he was.

Yes, just the way I am. The new me. The powerful new me.

But he lied, of course. "Anything and everything. I just want to get better, you know?"

PA Cheryl nodded and checked his chart. "Well, it looks like you can have a regular diet again. I'll see if I can get you something special from the cafeteria."

"Thank you, Cheryl."

PA Cheryl Parker entered notes on the computer. Stetson was still handcuffed to his hospital bed. He knew he had the power to break them, but he thought there was an easier way.

She turned to go, but David stopped her. "Cheryl?"

"Yes?" She faced him again.

"I hate to bother you, but..."

"What? What is it?"

David Stetson glanced sheepishly down to his handcuffs. "It's not really a big deal. But my wrist is chafed. Can you just look at it?"

"Well, that's not good," said PA Cheryl as she knelt down to take a look.

David Stetson, CREW scientist and top clearance Agent, grabbed her jaw and held it with his left cuffed hand. He tore his right hand from its clasp and reached over to choke her.

PA Cheryl looked up at him in pain and surprise as her jaw snapped. Terror and panic changed her expression from disbelief to panic when he grasped her neck. She struggled a minute or more, but he was strong now. So strong. He held her neck, squeezing harder and harder, until she quit struggling.

David Stetson's amplified strength allowed him to lift her limp body on top of him. He wanted to feed, yes. But he couldn't afford it now. He searched her pockets and found the keys to his freedom.

★ ★ ★

Moments later, Stetson emerged from his room dressed as a janitor. The guards outside nodded to him. Janitors often came and went; the guards didn't keep track of them. They were assigned to watch Stetson, after all. Not janitors. David Stetson used PA Cheryl's smock to carry an array of blood vials. They let him pass.

★ ★ ★

Stetson slipped silently up to one of the two guards stationed outside the Agent in Black's office/hospital room. He'd commandeered a fire extinguisher from a hallway and, without hesitation, brought it down hard at the back of the guard's head. Fully utilizing his heightened reflexes, he simultaneously pulled the guard's semi-automatic from his hip holster, and before the second guard could turn around, David Stetson shot him behind his right ear.

★ ★ ★

Dr. Robert Kaplan heard the commotion.

He panicked and ignored protocol. The Agent in Black was extremely ill, yes, but Kaplan took it upon himself to open the office door.

Mercifully, Kaplan died instantaneously from the bullet Stetson put between his eyes.

The infected scientist knew there was no time to waste. He crossed the room, lifted the Agent in Black onto his shoulders, and jumped through the office window.

CHAPTER TWENTY-SIX

We were in the basement.

I watched as my brother and friend devoured two heaping plates of top sirloin, hash browns, eggs and toast. Jared and Anna weren't too far behind, wolfing theirs down as well. Just one big, freaky family eating in the basement with two of its guests handcuffed to support beams.

I even sat down in the cellar and enjoyed Carla's great breakfast. Until now, I hadn't realized just how hungry I was.

Anna sat at the bottom of the stairs, peppering her Uncle Joe and Mike with questions about their well-being. Carla and I listened carefully to their answers, but the two Navy men revealed little. Yes, they were feeling better. Yes, they felt a little weird still, but also super alive. Mike let it slip that he felt stronger than ever, which I should have taken as a good sign, but for some reason, it didn't sit well with me. Mostly because, a few hours ago he didn't look fine. He looked murderous.

When Anna was satisfied about their well-being, she started in with a discussion of the space rock. I was pretty sure they told her the truth. Their story was wild, yes, but it made sense.

After breakfast, Carla and I coordinated a trip to the showers for the two LCs. They were filthy, and it was the least we could do. Anna couldn't watch as we took them back to the cellar, but she blew her uncle a kiss and he caught it, smiling.

I decided that I'd missed enough work. I certainly didn't feel like working, but I kept my sickness to myself, for now. Also, I knew that someone would put two-and-two together if Anna and Jared didn't soon show up at the zoo where they both worked and studied.

I promised my brother I'd be back in a few hours, and with more food. He smiled, I thought, a bit too cheerily. Either way, I felt like crap leaving them down there in the basement.

He still wasn't right. Something was off. I had to be sure he was safe.

Worst brother ever, I thought, as I locked up the house.

Since Carla's personal car was parked a few blocks away, we parted ways at the driveway, and Anna, Jared and I would hike back up to the observatory. I was tempted to give Carla a hug, but two things stopped me: one, my own awkwardness in front of my daughter, and, two, the fact that I wasn't feeling well.

After all, whatever I had, I didn't want to give it to Carla.

* * *

The morning was cool and sunny.

Almost too sunny. I averted my eyes, wishing I had remembered to grab my sunglasses. Birds filled the surrounding trees, twittering loudly. A strong scent of juniper filled the air. I loved juniper. As we hiked, we went over our story should anyone ask. We were all getting over some kind of bug. In a way, this was the truth. Anna agreed not to talk with any more government agents if any approached. She promised to stay with Brice or any one of the other zoo employees, even while doing her homework.

* * *

It was a busy day for everyone.

Carla was emotionally exhausted, but thankful that she had a day shift. She had a feeling she'd be at Jack Carter's that night. Despite the crazy circumstances, he was growing on her. Big time.

Anna had some work to do at the zoo. She really wanted to go to the observatory, but she'd been given the responsibility of cleaning some of the snakes' environments. She loved snakes, although Jared did not. He'd gone home to shower and change, making her promise him not to do anything stupid. For once, she kept her promise.

It was a good thing for her that she did.

★ ★ ★

I worked a long day inspecting various grounds at both the zoo and the observatory. I also took the time to check my simple living quarters at both places. Both places seemed undisturbed. But that really didn't mean anything, did it? Not when you were dealing with elite government agents.

Mostly, I felt watched. Maybe it was paranoia, or lack of sleep, or both. I was also feeling progressively worse, and it was all I could do to finish my shift.

I ate ravenously, despite my sickness. It may have been paranoia, too, that cautioned me to use cash. People were tracked all the time by credit card usage, weren't they?

★ ★ ★

Joe and Mike had waited just long enough for everyone to leave the house in Los Feliz. Then Joe pulled a couple of bobby pins out of his pocket that he'd swiped while showering. Years ago, he'd studied to be a locksmith before joining the military. As Joe liked to tell people: *there were no locked doors.* At least, not with him around. Five minutes later, sweat dripping from his brow, the handcuffs snapped off.

He did the same for Mike, and the two were gone before Lieutenant Commander Joseph Carter's older brother came back to check on them.

CHAPTER TWENTY-SEVEN

I left my truck at the observatory and hiked down.

Yes, I liked hiking down from the observatory. It cleared my head after a long day of work. And it wasn't so far that it was exhausting, but it was just long enough to unwind and enjoy nature. I was a park ranger for a reason. I loved being outdoors, immersing myself in the natural world. Except the hike now seemed to take longer than usual. At one point, I actually thought I was lost.

Lost? On trails I had hiked for years?

Anyway, when I got home, the cellar was empty, and the handcuffs were scattered on the ground. They'd been opened. Next to them, I saw the twisted bobby pin.

Joseph, of course. *Shit.*

Holding my gun with both hands, I worked my way through my house, checking rooms. But they were gone—probably long gone.

God, I was tired. I had to think logically, clearly. I poured about a third of a cup of instant coffee into a mug of water. I drank it down and forced it to stay down. If the coffee didn't do the trick, nothing legal would.

Anna would be devastated. I paced in my kitchen, feeling like shit, and feeling stupid that my brother had duped me. Then again, what had I expected? I'd locked him up like a goddamn criminal.

I continued pacing, running my hand through my hair. I felt awful, worse than I had in some time.

Where had my brother gone? We were in the hills of Los Feliz, just a hop, skip and jump from Los Angeles. They could be anywhere.

And they were infected. They were still sick.

My every instinct told me they'd put on a show for me. Christ, I was an idiot. Meanwhile, I wasn't thinking straight myself. They needed help, except I hadn't figured out how to help them. No one had found an antidote, not yet anyway. Not from the reports I was hearing.

And they were wanted.

Yes, it had been better to keep them on the down low. Maybe they could ride out the sickness. Maybe all of this would blow over.

Or maybe the world was going to hell in a hand basket.

It was late evening. I'd had a long day. I would have been tired anyway. Today, I'd found a pot farm in the back woods, which we were going to wipe clean later in the week. I'd also found a dead deer. It had been thoroughly mangled, and that had concerned me. It had been torn from limb to limb, and eaten. In particular, something had cracked its skull open, and eaten its...

I shook my head and shuddered and, for some damn reason...

My stomach growled.

What the hell was wrong with me?

Yes, my brother and friend had needed help, except they were wanted and were dangerous and I had made an executive decision to keep them hidden and safe from hurting themselves and others.

But they had gotten better. Yes, they had.

And they had fooled me.

Perhaps they were better.

Perhaps.

But I doubted it.

I needed to tell Anna that her uncle was gone, but not over the phone. My daughter just wasn't stable enough to hear this over the phone. Hell, I wasn't feeling very stable either. And I wasn't thinking clearly either.

I started to text Anna to meet me at the observatory, but checked that thought. Right now I didn't want her wandering anywhere by herself. Not even with Jared. Instead, I texted that I'd pick her up in an hour. If I hurried, I could make it.

I filled a couple of water bottles, grabbed my flashlight, and headed back out to the trails.

★ ★ ★

Lieutenant Commander Joseph Carter still had good intentions.

Joey, as his family called him, would beat this thing, whatever it was. He turned up the radio in the car he'd stolen. Laughed. It was kind of ironic that he'd learned how to hotwire a car in the Navy. The Navy had prepared him for a lot and disciplined him in ways he never would have on his own. He'd been rewarded, promoted for his excellent skills and performance. And he knew his best shot at getting better was to turn himself in. He was sick, contaminated. He knew, could feel it. But he didn't care, and as the minutes piled up, he cared less and less. About himself...or others.

No, that was not quite true. He still cared enough to keep fighting this. At least, a small part of him wanted to keep fighting.

The other part of him, well, it wanted to feed.

And—he swallowed hard—it wanted to kill. Yes, to kill and feed on fresh meat. Human meat. Yes, human meat sounded perfect. Just perfect.

What's wrong with me? Good God, what's wrong with me?

Too bad that Mike wouldn't come. Joey had a bad feeling about his friend. But it was too late now. Joey only hoped that Mike didn't do too much damage. He believed Mike's promise to stay away from Jack and Anna. As they parted ways on that quiet street, Mike had said he would take his own chances. There wasn't anything Joe could do about that now.

Onward and upward.

Joey found himself stuck in a sig-alert on the 5 Freeway going south. He grew impatient. He was hungry. He drummed his fingers on the steering wheel. He wanted to get out of the goddamn car, walk over to the closest vehicle on the freeway, reach inside and...

Joey smiled...then frowned.

Calm down, calm down.

He decided to pull off the freeway and eat. Yes, good choice. Luckily, he'd taken enough cash from his brother's nightstand for gas and a little food.

He parked at a Carl's Jr. Maybe a six-dollar burger would help, but he doubted it. Entering the place, Joe sniffed. He smelled burgers, fries, meat. Lots of meat.

Human meat.

Shit.

His olfactory registered something new. People. Standing in line, he hungrily sniffed the woman in front of him. She gave him an irritated glance. Joe backed off, concerned now. The urge was becoming stronger. Jesus. He gripped his hands behind his back. He'd planned on eating inside the diner, but his senses were too sharp right now. So were his cravings. He ordered, grabbed his bag, his drink and ate in the car.

The freeway was still stop-and-go. Joe felt a slight headache coming on. He still felt good. *Just as long as I can stay away from people,* he thought. He had debated leaving a note for his brother, then finally decided against it. What was he going to say, anyway? "Hey, it was nice being locked up in your cellar, big brother. Let's do it again sometime."

He still had his phone in his jacket pocket. He drummed his fingers and considered calling his brother now. Surely, both phones were being monitored. Should he risk a call? Were they actually listening to his calls? Did they really care that much about him, in particular? Surely there were others infected like him. Maybe they had bigger fish to fry.

Finally, after a half-hour of internal debate, he called. Jack answered on the first ring. He sounded winded. "Joey?"

"Yeah, it's me, bro."

"Where the hell are you? Christ, are you okay?"

"I'm fine, Jack. I'm on my way to the Seal Beach Base."

"The base? Joey, are you sure?"

"I'm pretty sure. I don't know what else to do, big bro. I'm not all the way better. You don't know what it's like."

As he drove, Joey heard Anna in the background, asking to talk with him.

"Put Anna on. Please, Jack."

There was a pause, and Joey knew his brother was debating the request. A moment later, he heard: "Uncle Joey?"

"Hey, sweetie. How's my girl? I'm sorry I scared you."

"It's okay, Uncle Joey! You're turning yourself in?"

"Yeah. I figure it's the best thing to do."

"Can we come see you?"

"I don't know, honey. Maybe not for a while." *Maybe never,* he thought.

"I love you," she choked. "Here, my dad wants to talk to you."

Jack came on. "Is Mike with you?"

"No. he's on his own."

"Well, where the hell is he?"

"I don't know where he went. But he promised to leave you alone."

Joey knew his brother was pissed, but Park Ranger Jack got it together. "You're really turning yourself in?"

"I am."

There was a pause. It was a very heavy, pregnant pause. Joey knew the implications, and so did his brother: There was a very good chance they might never see each other again.

"Be careful, Joey."

"I will."

"Love you, man."

"Love you, too."

Joey didn't blame his brother for being mad. Yes, it had been a bad idea to just let Mike go. Then again, it had been a very bad idea to check out the space rock.

Bad idea after bad idea, he thought, and drove on, the hunger within him growing stronger and stronger with each passing mile.

Very, very strong.

* * *

David Stetson wrapped his jacket around his hand and broke the little glass pane. He looked around again. The neighborhood was quiet. He reached inside and unlocked the back door.

"Come on," he said softly to the Agent in Black.

Agent Cole followed him inside. Stetson guided him to the oversized couch. "Lay down."

Cole complied. The Agent's symptoms were progressing, but he was still aware—aware that Stetson had tried to kill him, but now he was trying to save Cole's life. Why?

The curtains were drawn in the little cottage in Sunset Beach. Now, more than a few hundred yards away, they could hear the waves rushing. Tranquil, peaceful. Then why did the sound of it make Cole, somehow, even sicker? Although thirsty as hell, the thought of any water made him feel sick. Cole wondered why.

"Where are we?" he asked.

"This is a friend's place. She's out of town. No one will find us here."

"You sure about that?"

"She's...a girlfriend. No one knows of our relationship. Not the Navy, not my wife. No one. Yes, we're safe here."

Cole grunted.

"Look, you're going to get worse," Stetson said. "A lot worse. But then you'll get better."

Cole thought about that, then asked, "Why did you bring me with you?"

Stetson checked the kitchen for food. Cole wouldn't feel the ravenous hunger for another day, but Stetson was starving. He tried convincing himself that his craving for flesh—human flesh—would go away. Except the problem was, he almost wished the craving wouldn't go away. Not until he tried some. Or tried a lot.

Insane, he thought, going through the cupboards. *I'm going insane.*

He said to Cole, "I brought you with me because you're like me now."

"You tried to kill me."

He was scanning the meat compartment in his girlfriend's refrigerator. Jesus, what was her name? Stetson couldn't remember. He said, "Yeah, sorry about that. I wasn't thinking straight. Now, I'm making up for it. I feel a lot better."

"What do you mean?"

He irritably slammed the empty meat tray. Upon further scavenging, he came across a can of chili. Meat. Not a lot of it, granted, but it had some.

Better than nothing, he thought, and fetched a can opener.

A few minutes later, Stetson was sitting across from Cole, the open can of chili before him. The former Agent in Black showed no signs of hunger, although the scientist knew that would change soon enough. Soon, the hunger would be nearly overwhelming, followed by a period of near madness, and then...calm.

Stetson grinned and ate. Yes, he felt great. He almost felt normal, if not for the fact that he felt so goddamn strong.

And hungry.

As he ate, Stetson considered the Agent in Black before him. Soon his old boss would be in that horrible state of hunger and madness. Temporary madness, as Stetson had discovered. Now, the scientist wondered how he was going to contain the man. Well, he would worry about it later. For now, he was hungry as hell.

He said, "I mean I feel great. But I can't get enough to eat. I'm strong, though. Stronger than before."

"But your eyes..."

"Yeah, I know. Maybe that will go away, too."

Cole leaned back into the pillow. "Maybe."

"I'm thinking we need more information," said Stetson.

"Well, that's what we were doing," Cole grumbled, "when you decided to take a bite out of me."

Stetson shrugged. Truth was, that was the best bite of anything he'd had in some time.

Yeah, I'm a monster, he thought, and nearly grinned.

Cole was thinking about what he was about to become—what he would inevitably become. So little was known. It had happened so quickly. The best scientists were on it, but now he and Stetson were not privy to the latest findings. Yes, they needed more information—and fast.

Mostly, Cole was thinking about how Stetson had attacked him. God, the man had been so strong. The Agent in Black hoped that that stage of illness and infection would be temporary for him as well.

"Knowledge is power," Stetson added.

Cole nodded. "Well, knock yourself out." He closed his reddening eyes.

"I have an idea," said Stetson after a moment.

Cole waited, eyes still closed. His mind fuzzy, thoughts chaotic. *God help me.*

Stetson continued, "What about the ones that got away?"

"Carter and Mendoza?"

"Yeah, them," said Stetson. And he told Cole his plan. Cole, despite feeling like hell, grinned.

It was a hell of a plan.

★ ★ ★

The 605 Freeway was finally clearing up when Joey's cell phone rang. His heart skipped a beat with the hope of his brother contacting him. The call was from a restricted number.

His brain was feeling fuzzy again. He knew he shouldn't pick up, but decided to anyway.

"Hello?" he said. Even to his own ears, Joey noticed his voice sounded harsh, almost guttural.

"Don't hang up," said a voice.

It was him, thought Joey. *The Agent in Black.*

"I want to talk to you."

"Then talk."

"Where are you?"

"Never mind that."

"I can have the phone traced."

"Then I'll toss it out the window."

"You are driving."

"Yes."

"Where?"

Lieutenant Commander Joseph Carter considered the question, then said. "I'm going to turn myself in."

"And Lieutenant Mendoza?"

"He's on his own."

"Where?"

"I honestly don't know."

"Very well. I don't want you to turn yourself in. Not yet."

"What do you mean?"

And the Agent in Black told Joey the plan. A few minutes later, Joe Carter got off the freeway and, instead of heading to the naval base, he continued on toward Sunset Beach.

CHAPTER TWENTY-EIGHT

It had been a helluva day.

Earlier, my brother, Joey, had turned himself in—although he'd let his infected friend run off.

Worst idea ever, I thought.

Exhausted and feeling increasingly ill, I'd gone to bed early to try to sleep it off. But sleep never really came, and my chaotic dreams were weird, filled with frightening images. Bloody images. I was a killer in my dreams. Unstoppable, uncontrollable.

Jesus, I thought as I lay on my simple cot in the small room that connected to the equally small living room, where I heard the TV on. I checked the time. Just after midnight. I checked my texts. Carla had news. She was coming right over. That had been twenty minutes ago.

I swung out of bed and plodded out to the kitchen.

"You look like hell," said my daughter.

"I love you, too."

I made some coffee. My head felt dull and sluggish. The cut on my hand felt inflamed. I ignored my hand and concentrated on the coffee.

I hadn't heard from Joey since he'd told me he was turning himself in, but neither had I expected to. For all I knew, my poor brother was strapped to a medical table somewhere, being poked and prodded and tested. That thought alone made me feel sick. I reassured myself that he had made the right choice. At the very least, he wouldn't be shot by some trigger-happy cop. And, hopefully, they would give him real help. Perhaps they had already found a cure.

I sat in a recliner next to Anna. I was about to sip my coffee when my stomach turned. I set the cup aside, suddenly nauseous.

"You okay?" Anna asked.

I nodded. No, I wasn't, but she didn't need to know that. She had enough to worry about these days. I said, "Anything on the news?"

"About the outbreak? Nothing."

I figured it would be only a matter of time before the news about the infection and space rocks would spread. It was hard to keep infected people under wraps.

With Joey now turned in, a very big part of me just wished that this whole damn thing would blow over. Or go away. But my own sickness made that impossible. The burning in my hand made that impossible.

I pushed aside the thought and got up and looked out of the kitchen's small window. It was late and Los Feliz was quiet.

Headlights shone around the corner. Carla was here. "Anna, I'll just be right outside."

"That's fine."

I hesitated. "Are you going to be okay?"

She rolled her eyes. "Geez, Dad. I'll be right here. No one's gonna come get me." She went back to flipping through the TV channels.

She was right, of course. I stepped outside just as Carla got out of her patrol car. She looked beautiful in the moonlight. I was about to hug her, when I stopped and dropped my hands to my side.

"What, no hug?" teased Carla. She smiled, but I saw the slight hurt look on her face.

"I'm not, ah, feeling well," I said.

"The flu?" She was about to reach up and touch my cheek, when I pulled back. "Maybe it's better not to touch me."

"I hardly think—"

"Please don't," I said.

And now I thought that Carla caught the urgent tone in my voice, and perhaps even the hidden meaning. She stared at me for a long moment, then reached down to my hand, where I had received the cut after punching Mike the day before.

She lifted my hand up and studied it closely. The cut was far, far worse. The skin around it was red and swollen. Bluish veins had begun spreading away from the cut.

The color drained from her face. "Where did you get this cut, Jack?"

I didn't say anything. My brain felt cloudy. Thoughts seemed impossible to form. In fact, they were getting harder and harder to form as the hours piled up.

"You're infected, Jack. One of them bit you."

"He didn't bite me." I explained to her about the punch, the bloody lip, the cut from a tooth.

"Jack..."

I held up a hand. "I don't want to talk about it. Not now."

"When? When you're attacking your own daughter? Me? When you're chained in your own cellar?"

"I don't know what to do, Carla."

"You need help."

"From who?"

"We'll find you help."

"We will, I promise." I wanted to change the subject. A part of me wanted to to ignore the problem altogether. Except that wasn't me, of course. I never ignored problems. Hell, I made a living as a park ranger by seeing problems and fixing them,.

What's wrong with me?

I inhaled and, before Carla could say anything else, I said, "Why did you come tonight?"

"Jack, you can't just pretend—"

"I'm not pretending anything, Carla. Just not right now, please."

She studied me, studied my hand, then reluctantly said, "It's about your brother."

My heart literally jolted. "What about my brother?"

"Have you talked to him yet?"

"No, not since he was about to turn himself in. Why?"

Carla took a deep breath, held my gaze. "There's still an APB out on them."

"Wait, why? He turned himself in."

"Jack, he never did. I pulled a couple of strings. A friend who knows who's who at the base checked it out. Your brother's still missing."

That hit me hard. Jesus, all this time I thought my brother was in a medical facility, or at least in custody. Where could he be?

"I'm sorry," she offered quietly.

I wiped a hand over my face, rubbed my neck. It had been hell these past few shitty days. "Not your fault," I said.

How was I going to tell Anna? Looking up into the heavens, I realized I might be staring at the genesis of our problem down here on our little Earth. It made me feel a little inconsequential.

"You want to come in? Maybe we can talk Anna into a game of Scrabble." *That is*, I thought, *before I tell her that her uncle has gone missing.*

"I wish I could," she answered. "But I'm on duty. Jack, your hand..."

"I know," I said.

"You need to get help."

"I will," I said. She looked at me for a long moment. She seemed about to touch me, and paused. I wanted her to touch me, needed her to touch me.

"Good idea," I said. "I don't want you to get sick."

And then she surprised the hell out of me by standing up on her tiptoes and kissing me softly on the cheek. "I'll take my chances," she said, whispering in my ear.

I could still feel her soft lips on my cheek as I watched her drive away.

CHAPTER TWENTY-NINE

Anna was catching up on some sleep.

Good for her. I wish I could have said the same for myself. She'd taken the news about her uncle pretty hard. I wanted to hug her, to hold her close, to reassure her that everything would be okay.

But I couldn't do that. I couldn't risk touching her, not with my infected wound, a wound I had now doused with a few bottles of alcohol and a handful of penicillin I had swiped from the zoo's veterinary supplies.

I was surprised to see that the wound was getting worse, the darker veins spreading over the back of my hand.

She'd finally cried herself to sleep, while I sat listening in the living room, scanning the news for anything regarding the outbreak. Nothing at all.

I opened and closed my hand. The wound burned in a way that I'd never experienced before. In a way, it seemed to be growing hotter.

I should have been terrified...but I wasn't. I should be running to the doctor—any doctor.

But I wasn't.

Apathy filled me. Disinterest. Fatigue. I just wanted to sit here and do...

Nothing.

All the while, my hand got progressively worse. All the while, I knew in my heart and soul that I had what my brother and friend had. What the people on the Internet had.

I'm sick, I thought. *Infected.*

And yet...and yet, I didn't give a damn.

No, I *did* give a damn.

Fight it, I thought. *Fight it goddammit. Do something. Anything.*

I forced myself up out of the recliner. A monumental effort. I considered what to do next. I knew I needed to see a doctor. At least, I needed to head straight for the closest Center for Disease Control.

I was diseased. Very, very diseased.

Shit.

Maybe it will go away. After all, Joey and Mike seemed better. They seemed alert and healthy.

Maybe, I thought. But they also seemed...different, too. At least, Joey did. I didn't know Mike well enough to know the difference.

Joey had seemed...not entirely there. As if he were moving on auto pilot, perhaps. There but not there.

I stood there in my living room and considered what to do...and finally opted for some fresh air...but before I did, I automatically checked the gun at my hip. No, I didn't often wear my ranger-issued Colt .45 around the house. Then again, extreme times called for extreme measures.

I headed into the back yard.

* * *

He was on the hillside above the row of beautiful homes, watching, waiting, growing hungrier...and angrier.

* * *

I inhaled the night air deeply, filling my lungs and wondered how much longer I would enjoy such deep breaths.

I'm sick, dying.

That I was sick, I now had no doubt. But dying? I didn't know that. That I might lose my mind, well, that was another matter entirely. My brother was here, but not here. A *part* of him was here.

My hand burned, throbbed. I felt it slowly spreading, inching over my skin.

Where did the infection come from? Space? An alien attack? Or something that's meant to look like an alien attack?

I didn't know, I only knew that I was feeling simultaneously thirsty and repulsed by the thought of water. And angry. A nearby buzzing insect was working my last nerve.

It's not me, I thought. *I don't get angry. Not that easily.*

So, I stood outside and looked into the night sky, only lightly speckled with stars. Southern Californians were not privy to many stars. Too bad. The nearby koi pond, filled with fat, lumbering fish, gurgled softly.

I took in another breath, held it, and as I released it, I heard the rustling along the hillside.

* * *

Mike had no intention of leaving the Carters alone.

No, not when he caught the scent of the young one. He couldn't remember her name, nor did he care. The young girl, Joey's niece. The daughter of the son-of-a-bitch who had locked him up.

Park ranger or not, that motherfucker was going to pay, and he was going to pay dearly.

So, Lieutenant Commander Michael Mendoza had waited for his one-time buddy to head off in his own direction, and then Mike had circled back into the woods...and waited.

He grew hungrier and hungrier and, for reasons he no longer cared about, angrier and angrier.

* * *

It was nippy enough that I could see my breath.

It was one of those rare, super-clear nights. The moonlight gently cast silver rays on the surrounding trees and over the rugged hillside, which was crowded with spruce, cedar, firs and a dozen or more different pine species.

The rustling came again, just beyond the backyard fence. There wasn't much beyond the fence other than a lot of woods and trails that led up to the observatory. As I well knew, all sorts of critters filled these woods, from coyotes to squirrels to skunks. I sniffed the air. Not a skunk.

Probably a cottontail, I thought.

I'd given up smoking years ago, but I sure as hell could have used one now. Just a smoke. Not a drink. For some reason, the thought of anything liquid turned my stomach. And yet...my mouth was damned dry.

So weird, I thought.

The sound came again, closer this time. In fact, it might have been just behind the backyard wall. There wasn't much back there, other than a lot of hillside, trees and God knew what else.

Again, I automatically checked my firearm. Hell, any good cop would.

And, yes, park rangers were cops, too. Just not as cool.

The rustling sound had my full attention, and I tried to imagine what it could be. This last noise was closer to a grate, as in rocks grating over dirt. A big sound. Too big for a cottontail.

Deer? We had those here, although not many.

I'd worked in these forests for fifteen years now and little, if anything, made me nervous. I even knew how to stand down a mountain lion. It took nerves of steel, yes, but I had done it on a few occasions.

Why I felt the need to remove the Colt .45 from the holster, I didn't know. Cop instinct, maybe. Nerves maybe. It wasn't every day that meteorites crashed to Earth and infected humans with a bizarre illness. It wasn't every day that one heard stories of people eating other people.

Either way, gun in hand, I crept toward the backyard fence, gun held before me.

* * *

Lieutenant Commander Michael Mendoza was having an extremely difficult time controlling himself, especially now that someone had exited the home and stood not more than fifty feet away.

Mendoza's fingers curled.

Before this, he had always been a patient man. Hell, the military demanded it. As a lieutenant commander in the Navy, it would take weeks to reach destinations. Sometimes, his ship would be out to sea for nine months at a time.

And yet, now...

Now he couldn't control himself. He felt so powerful. So god-damned powerful. Like he could do anything. Like he could easily leap this six-foot wall. In fact, he was sure he could.

He stood in the bushes and tuned his ears toward whoever had come outside. The person had been standing there, but now, he was coming toward Mendoza.

He was just on the other side of the wall.

Mike's curling fingers formed fists...and now he was running toward the fence, picking up speed, running faster than he'd ever run before. He was powerful beyond all reason.

He leaped high into the air—

CHAPTER THIRTY

I hadn't gotten halfway across the big backyard when I next heard the sound of running feet.

Not hooves, not paws...but running.

Human running.

Perhaps even more strange, the sound appeared to be coming toward me—

A shape appeared over my fence, leaping high into the clear night air—

"Holy shit!"

I swung my weapon up.

* * *

Mike was airborne.

Wind rushed over him as he arched high above the stone fence. God, he felt powerful, unstoppable.

Down below, he saw the man—the source of Mike Mendoza's unrelenting fury. The man who had locked him up like a goddamned animal.

The park ranger.

The soon-to-be-dead park ranger.

As Mike braced for his landing, he wondered how the bastard would taste—

* * *

I couldn't have been more shocked.

I'd expected to spook at most, a deer. Perhaps even a bum. I hadn't expected this. No one could have.

I didn't shoot, mostly because I hadn't a clue what was happening, who was leaping over the fence, who was descending down upon me.

Had I known, I would have fired and kept firing until my weapon was empty.

As the flying figure descended rapidly, the moonlight caught his features. Interestingly, the first thing I saw were the red eyes.

No, he was not my brother. The flying figure was his Navy pal.

Where he had come from, I hadn't a clue. How he had gotten airborne, I didn't know either. It took all I had to dive to one side as the son-of-a-bitch came down on me.

As it was, his boots caught my shoulder and knocked me down hard into the back yard's soft grass.

The blow was harder than anything I'd felt perhaps ever in my life. I felt as if a car had hit me. A car with combat boots.

I was too busy tumbling and skidding on my face to see what he had done, but before I could regain my senses, he was standing over me. His face was in shadow, except for those red eyes.

I had just enough time to think: *Jesus, is that what I'm going to look like*, before he picked me up off the ground by my collar, held me before him, and drove his fist hard into my face.

The burst of light in my skull bloomed magnificently. The burst of pain, not so much. Once again, I found myself tumbling head over ass in the very back yard where I had so often played catch with Anna...and barbequed our dinners.

From upstairs, above the hulking figure who was reaching for me yet again, I saw a light turn on.

A window opened.

A head popped out.

"Dad!" screamed Anna.

Lieutenant Commander Mike Mendoza swung his head up and looked, and smiled. I saw the son-of-a-bitch smile. And I saw the hungry look in his crimson eyes. It was the same look I'd seen earlier.

As if I didn't exist, the bastard turned and headed for my house. He was stronger than anything I'd ever come across, and that included some wild animals.

He had me beat on strength, yes, but not on training.

You see, I was taught to never, ever let my weapon out of my sight, and I hadn't now.

I was still holding it, even as the bastard had been pummeling me.

I was still doubled over in the grass when I yelled, "Hey, fucker!"

Mendoza paused in a pool of silver moonlight, turned and looked toward me, his eyes flashing red, when I pulled the trigger. The shot, I was certain, caught him in the upper chest. I pulled the trigger again, missed. A brick exploded on the back wall of the old home.

I pulled the trigger again, and might have caught him in the arm. Either way, Mendoza pitched face-first into the gurgling koi pond.

CHAPTER THIRTY-ONE

Mike's body was still, face down in the water.

I realized that Anna had witnessed this. Oh, God. I looked up at her and saw something else that briefly startled me—not as much as a man flying over the fence—but startled me nonetheless. Jared was with her in her bedroom, looking out through her bedroom window.

They both ducked in as I picked myself up out of the grass. My fingers still gripped the weapons tightly. As I finally found my shaking feet, my daughter and her boyfriend appeared in the back yard, rushing through the back door.

They both looked at the Navy man lying face first in the water, and then my daughter broke free from Jared and ran over to me. "Daddy, are you all right?" She looked at the gun in my hand, and then saw my hand for the first time. The wound, after all, was bigger, now more than ever. And seemingly spreading faster.

"Your hand, Daddy!"

"I know, baby."

"Are you okay?"

"Of course, baby."

"But your hand—"

"Let's not worry about that now."

I hugged her. She was crying. Hell, I felt like crying, too. Jared—who had a little bit of crazy in him—had gone over to Mike and turned the man over. I was about to shout to him to not touch the man, but realized that if there was a chance to save him, then we should.

He was, after all, sick.

Like me.

My shoulder hurt like a son of a bitch where his boots had driven home. If possible, my hand hurt even more. Sudden images whirled through my mind. Thoughts of chaining up my little brother and this guy. Who would do that for me? I suddenly staggered. I couldn't help it. I gently pushed Anna away, bent over and vomited.

When I was done retching, I had sudden clarity. I was sick, infected by the same disease that had stricken my brother and his friend. I just witnessed a man leap over a six-foot wall as easy as if it had been a street curb—a man who was hell-bent on either killing me or coming after my daughter. Or both.

With the reports of the infected eating people, nothing was ever going to be the same.

Ever.

My neighbors would have heard the gunshot. It wouldn't have gone unnoticed. The police would come. They would find the body. A full investigation would ensue. I would be questioned about everything, even harboring a fugitive. I would lose my job, and possibly get arrested. And they would see the infection. I might never go to a jail. I would probably disappear like my brother.

I would disappear off the face of the Earth.

I could think of only one answer: to run.

"Anna, listen to me," I said. I know I wasn't thinking straight. My brain felt sluggish, drugged, sick. I tried again. "Anna, we have to get out of here. Jared, I'm sorry you're in the middle of this. And what the hell are you doing here anyway...in my daughter's bedroom?"

"Anna didn't want to be alone—"

I shook my head. "Never mind that. I want you to go home and forget what you saw."

He took Anna's hand firmly. "I'm not going anywhere, sir."

I wasn't expecting him to put up a fight. But he loved my daughter, I could see that. I was just about to argue with him, when I heard a curious sound coming from the koi pond.

It was a cough.

* * *

He spurted water and rolled to his side, coughing.

"Get back," I ordered the kids and lifted my gun again.

Mendoza coughed again and again, and now water and blood bubbled up from his mouth. He coughed some more and gasped. I suspected that a lung had been shot through.

As I cautiously approached, he turned his pale face toward me and looked up. "Jack?" he said, or, at least, I think he said my name. His voice was harsh and guttural.

I aimed the gun at his face, lining up between his eyes, when I noticed something about just that...his eyes.

They weren't red. Sure, they were still kind of red...but not the flaming red that I had seen just five minutes earlier.

"Wait, Jack," he said, and sounded a little more clear.

I paused.

"Jack. Please don't shoot me—" He sat up—or tried to. He grimaced and reached for the wound in his chest. Blood was spreading rapidly.

I kept the gun on him, my muddled brain confused as hell.

"Dad, wait," Anna said. "Don't you see? His eyes. He's better."

Mike looked from me to her. I realized that he was cognitive. In fact, much more cognitive than even earlier today. He did seem better. And, yes, the eyes...

"Dad, don't shoot him."

It was an absurd, insane sentence. My little girl asking me not to murder someone. And hadn't I just killed him? I mean, hadn't I just shot him in the chest and watched him drown? How long had he been face-first in the pond? Five minutes, surely.

Mike pressed a fist into his bleeding chest. I saw another wound on his arm where my bullet had grazed him. Mike looked alert, awake. But he was hurt. Yes. Damn hurt. Still, he seemed cognizant, aware. The glassy-eyed look was gone. This, I suspected, was the real Mike.

I lowered the gun as a police siren filled the night air.

CHAPTER THIRTY-TWO

It was later.

The police consisted of, thank God, Carla. She'd responded to a report of a shooting and, by the time we had explained the situation, she'd decided to report that I had shot at a coyote that had jumped into the back yard.

The zoo veterinarian, a man I trusted and knew well, was presently working on Mike. The vet had asked only if a crime had been committed. Other than trespassing, which I could live with, I told him no. That was all he needed to know and he went to work on the man.

I was feeling increasingly like shit. Not because I had suffered a minor beating, but because I was getting sicker and sicker.

We were all sitting around the kitchen table, Carla included.

"But *how* is he better?" Anna was asking. She had yet to take her eyes off me. She knew her daddy was sick and was doing all she could to be brave. God, I loved her.

I just couldn't lose her. Not like this.

The two young minds were doing the thinking for me, with Carla chiming in here and there. She looked at me, too. There was sadness in her eyes. Alarm, too. I didn't blame her. She should feel alarmed.

"Maybe the gunshot," suggested Jared. "Or maybe losing so much blood somehow cured him. You know, starve a cold, bleed a zombie."

I nearly laughed. It was the first that I had heard anyone at all say that word. So, that's what this was. Unfortunately, I was seeing my life from both sides of the zombie patrol. Currently, I was fighting them. Would I soon become one of them?

Earlier, I'd heard from Carla that more and more reports of the infected were making it into the mainstream media. Also being reported was that there was no known cure. Police were put on high alert. It would only be a matter of time before the world knew.

Jesus, how many were there? Hundreds? Thousands?

And, no doubt, they were multiplying at a frightening rate.

Soon, my brother, me and Mike would be nothing more than a blip on the government's radar. Soon, they would have a much bigger mess to deal with.

I saw my daughter's brain working as she took in all that surrounded her. Her wide, excited eyes tried to puzzle it all together. Finally, she snapped her fingers, actually snapped them like her mother used to do. I think it was the first time that I realized she was growing up.

"It's the water!" she exclaimed.

"What do you mean, honey?" asked Carla.

"It has to do with the water," she said again, more excited. She stepped over to me and took my hand. Not my bad hand, but my good hand. As she spoke, she looked into my eyes. "And if it could cure him, it can cure you, too. And Uncle Joe."

"Baby, we don't know if Mike is cured—"

"He's cured, Daddy. I know it."

I thought about that even as I wondered where the hell my brother was—I thought about that as the burning in my hand now crept over my wrist and up along my forearm.

A cure? Was it possible?

To be continued in:
Zombie Rage
Walking Plague Trilogy #2
Coming soon!

Also available:
Sharpened Edges
by Elizabeth Basque

Temple of the Jaguar
Nick Caine Series #1
by J.R. Rain
and Aiden James

ABOUT THE AUTHORS:

J.R. Rain is an ex-private investigator who now writes full-time. He lives in a small house on a small island with his small dog, Sadie, who has more energy than Robin Williams. Please visit him at www.jrrain.com.

Elizabeth Basque lives in southern California with her two children. She's the author of Sharpened Edges, the first in a paranormal mystery series. She's presently hard at work on her next novel.

CPSIA information can be obtained at www.ICGtesting.com
Printed in the USA
LVOW06s1833290715

448120LV00005B/328/P